The H
and
the Haunters

and other gothic tales

by

Edward Bulwer Lytton

edited with notes and introduction by
William Lawrence

Able Publishing

The Haunted and the Haunters
and other gothic tales

This edition©Knebworth Estates 2000

ISBN: 0 953711 62 5

Published in Great Britain by:
The Knebworth House Education and Preservation Trust
Knebworth House, Knebworth, Herts SG3 6PY
Tel: (01438) 812661   Fax: (01438) 811908
Website: www.knebworthhouse.com

Typesetting by:
Able Publishing
13 Station Road, Knebworth
Herts SG3 6AP
Tel: (01438) 814316 Fax: (01438) 812532
Website: www.ablepublishing.co.uk

PREFACE

My great great grandfather, Edward Bulwer Lytton, 1st Baron Lytton of Knebworth, was England's most popular author in the 1830s. He was above all a great storyteller. He was fascinated by the occult and the inner workings of the mind. He made a lifetime study of the spirit world and his stories helped shape the genre of the ghost story, as we know it.

Therefore I heartily welcome this new edition of a selection of his very best short stories. It is long overdue.

William Lawrence has gathered together these masterpieces from the literary periodicals of the time and from Bulwer Lytton's own novels. They will certainly stir the imagination and may well send shivers down the spine.

David Lytton Cobbold
2nd Baron Cobbold of Knebworth
Knebworth House, in the year 2000.

Born in 1972, William Lawrence was educated at Stamford School in Lincolnshire and the University of Newcastle-upon-Tyne, where he read Classics. He is a full time writer and journalist, currently living in Singapore where he works as editor of *Television Asia.*

CONTENTS

NOTE ON THE TEXTS

Edward Bulwer Lytton contributed to a variety of periodicals during his life and many of the tales printed in this volume, first appeared in magazines and were then later reprinted in book form. A collection of his work from *New Monthly,* along with a few other tales and essays of a similar style, were reproduced in *The Student.*

A Manuscript found in a Madhouse was one of two tales contributed to the *Literary Souvenir* in 1829 and was reprinted in the first edition of *The Student,* although it was dropped from later editions. The periodical version is the one printed here and it was signed: 'By the author of Pelham.'

The other tales collected in *The Student* are *Monos and Daimos, Arasmanes* and *Chairolas.* The first was originally published in *New Monthly* for May 1830, the second in *The Amulet* 1834 and the third in *Heath's Book of Beauty* 1836. All three versions here are from the 1875 Knebworth edition of *The Student.*

The Nymph of the Lurlei Berg was printed in *New Monthly* November 1832, signed 'Mitio', and *The Three Sisters* appeared in *Heath's Book of Beauty* 1838, 'Translated from the Phoenician by the author of "Eugene Aram" &c.' Both texts used here are taken from the original periodicals.

The Fallen Star and *The Life of Dreams* were both interpolated into the novel *The Pilgrims of the Rhine,* published in 1834 and the texts here are from the 1875 Knebworth edition. *The Haunted and the Haunters* was printed in *Blackwoods* 1859 and was originally a longer tale. The version here is the abridged version from the appendix to the New

Knebworth Edition of *The Pilgrims of the Rhine.* Bulwer abridged the tale himself and regarded this as the standard version.

The tales appear in order of composition and only minor errors have been slightly corrected; habitual idiosyncrasies of punctuation are retained.

NOTE ON THE ILLUSTRATIONS

Untitled engravings in this book are "Scenes from the Old Testament" by John Martin, inscribed to "E.L. Bulwer Esq. M.P. with the Artist's compliments" in 1833.

The image on the front cover is Edward Bulwer Lytton's death mask, 1873. Knebworth House collection. Photo: Kenneth Boone.

The back cover is Knebworth House (detail) by F.W Hulme, 1844. Edward Bulwer Lytton extended his mother's gothic adaptation of the Lytton family's Tudor home, with a fantastical aray of gargoyles and arabesques.

Edw Lytton Bulwer

INTRODUCTION

Our imagination kept rigidly from the world is the Eden in which we walk with God... We learn thus to make our dreams and thoughts our companions, our Egeria. We acquire the doctrine of self-dependence, self suffices to the self. In our sleep from the passions of the world, God makes Eve to us in our own breasts.

On the want of Sympathy

From a tender age Edward Bulwer[1] fed his eager imagination with tales of fantasy and wonder. Looking back in later life he noted the arrival of his grandfather's library at his mother's home in Baker Street, where it lodged temporarily on its way to the auction house, as the most significant event of his childhood. In his autobiography he wrote: 'Behold the great event of my infant life - my siege of Troy, my Persian Invasion, my Gallic revolution - the arrival of my grandfather's books.'

By the time he left Cambridge University in 1825 he had already enjoyed literary success of his own. The 1823-4 editions of *Knight's Quarterly* contained several pieces of his short fiction, including Narenor, which reveals an early fascination with the occult. The tale centres on a physically deformed youth's yearning to be loved, that leads to his search for the Elixir of Life, to grant him earthly beauty; and the Philosopher's Stone, to enable him to turn base metal into gold. The idea of a physically deformed youth yearning to be loved, which was imperative to the plot, prefigures A *Manuscript found in a Madhouse*, published in the *Literary*

---

[1] He added Lytton, his mother's name, to his own when he inherited Knebworth House from her in 1843. We shall refer to him here as Bulwer.

Souvenir in 1829, which in turn was the progenitor of a whole sub-genre of horror story.

Bulwer's interest in metaphysical study remained one of the few constants in his life, occasionally to the detriment of his literary career. His early novels, witty social satires like *Pelham* (1828) and *Paul Clifford* (1830) were widely read and instantly established him as one of the most popular authors of his time. His more philosophical works, however, like *Devereux* (1829), the public perceived as ostentatious and overburdened with literary reference. Bulwer admitted this failing, attributing the unpopularity of *Devereux* to over zealous experiments 'in the midst of metaphysical studies and investigations varied and miscellaneous enough, if not very deeply conned...'.

It was during this period that Bulwer penned *A Manuscript found in a Madhouse*, a macabre tale that helped establish a genre of horror fiction that endured throughout the 19th century. Bulwer may have found his fascination with the occult 'not very deeply conned', but as he stood at the portals of greater learning and fed his mind with the alchemical law of Paracelsus, the philosophical speculations of Descartes and countless other learned works, he delighted in his new found knowledge. His rising reputation led in 1829 to the offer of 20 guineas a sheet for contributions to the *New Monthly* magazine, in May 1830 he contributed his first piece of short fiction, *Monos and Daimos*.

The byronically moody story was a sharp contrast to its contemporary, the novel *Paul Clifford*. Whereas in *Paul Clifford* the criminal is gay and dashing, in this tale the criminal's conscience is branded with the mark of Cain. A dark, sinister allegory, it illustrates the more likely personal consequences of committing a heinous crime. Bulwer had been influenced by Thomas Hood's *Dream of Eugene Aram*, the true story of a Norfolk teacher, hanged for murder, whose plight he was to revisit in a later novel.

Bulwer's influence, in turn, was being felt. The American

master of the macabre Edgar Allen Poe was later to express his delight in *Monos and Daimos* and in a letter to T.H White, declared it an instance of, 'the ludicrous heightened into the grotesque; the fearful coloured into the horrible; the witty exaggerated into the burlesque; the singular wrought out into the strange and mystical'. He went on: 'You may say this is bad taste, I have my doubts about it.'

Bulwer took on the editorship of *New Monthly* in November 1831 and proceeded to publish a number of his short stories, includng a 10-part serial entitled *Asmodeus at Large*. Interpolated into the main story was another short story entitled *The Tale of Kosem Kosamin the Magician*. And while the moral of the tale was Christian, the rest was entirely occult, focusing on the desire to know the secrets of the universe, an important theme in another of his later novels.

In November 1832 he submitted *The Nymph of the Lurlei Berg*, another tale which indulged his taste for the fantastic. This embellished German folk-tale demonstrates Bulwer's enthusiasm for fairylands and magical kingdoms, and his taste for the philosophy and lore of Germany. The German literary style of the time was less cynical, more inclined to sentiment, than its English counterpart; and in a land that still told of spirits and elves, Bulwer's work was well received. *The Nymph* aroused little interest in England, as indeed did his next German tale, *The Pilgrims of the Rhine* (1834).

Published in 1834, although actually written in the summer of 1832, *The Pilgrims of the Rhine* tells of two lovers, Gertrude and Trevelyan, who along with Gertrude's father, Vane, conduct a journey up the river Rhine. Gertrude is dying and the tale serves a rich, emotional chronicle of the depth of the lovers' passions. It also provides a framework for the author to describe the history and folklore of the Rhine, through the mouths of the characters. During the story the hero Trevelyan narrates the *Life of Dreams* as an account of a man's attempt to survive in the world of dreams[1]; and later in the main story a student from Heidebern tells the story of *The Fallen Star*. In the *Life of Dreams* Bulwer muses on the metaphysical implications of escapism; and in *The Fallen Star* he attempts an early experiment in anthropology, exploring the beliefs of early man.

Alongside the story of Gertrude and Trevelyan runs a tale of fairies whose actions and adventures mirror events in the real world. Bulwer removes the barrier between the worlds, and with Pipalee and her fairy companions paints a merry picture of the elven world. The German market lapped it up; the English market was, at best, indifferent. The biographer Sadlier described it as, 'fondant-fiction at its worst devised for silly girls at Christmas time', and declared that 'it was of no more importance than the romanticised engravings around which it was written'. Bulwer had let his imagination run free, and this led him even further into the world of the supernatural.

In April 1833 the novel *Godolphin* appeared and although, to appease his public, much of the book has nothing to do with metaphysics, focusing on politics and the fashions of the day, the crux of events revolve around an astrological prophecy. Godolphin, the hero of the novel, becomes a pupil of the Danish astrologer Volktman. The stargazer casts a terrible horoscope for Godolphin, predicting a union with his young daughter, Lucilla, but also an early death. Volktman believes in the power of trance and in 'magnetism' and as the novel reaches its climax Lucilla, heiress to her father's lore, tells of the spirits who share our world: 'Dread Solemn Shadows... the night is their season as the day is ours; they march in the moonbeams and are borne upon the wings of the winds.'

---

[1] Bulwer was always fascinated by dreams and once wrote: 'In dreams commence all human knowledge. In dreams hovers over measureless space the world beyond.'

In July 1834, the public was given Bulwer's most enduring novel, *The Last Days of Pompeii*. This novel again employs a supernatural theme, albeit more frivolously, embodied in the esoteric wisdom of the anti-hero Arbaces, a licentious Egyptian magician. Arbaces is referred to as 'Hermes, Lord of the Flaming Belt', a reminder of Trismegistus Hermes, who is associated with a great deal of mystical lore.

The magical traditions of the ancient world were further developed by the "Chaldaean Seeker" in *Arasmenes*, published in *The Amulet* for 1834. In this adventurer, the hero prefigures Zanoni, the eponymous hero of his greatest occult fiction, published in 1842. A companion piece to *Arasmenes*, entitled *Chairolas*, appeared two years later in *Heath's Book of Beauty*. Another allegorical quest, this prefigures in its hero stumbling upon an enlightened city - Bulwer's final novel, the remarkable *The Coming Race* (1871), which was to become a landmark in the rising genre of science fiction.

Between *Chairolas* in 1836 and his death in 1873, Bulwer only authored six more pieces of short fiction. By the mid-1830s his marriage to Rosina Wheeler had become fabled as one of the most disastrous of the age. Eventual separation in 1836 reconciled him to his mother, and he inherited a fortune which, combined with sales of his novels, left him no longer in such need of funds. His output in periodicals, both fiction and otherwise, declined.

The Three Sisters followed *Chairolas*, appearing two years later in *Heath's Book of Beauty* for 1838. Beneath this light-hearted allegory is a good deal of bitterness aimed at society's mongering. His separation from Rosina had been both acrimonious and public. 'I tremble every day lest my domestic sores should be dragged still more into the light... and exposed to all that is most galling in public gossip', he writes in his diary for 1838. In the closing lines of *The Three Sisters*, he laments, 'as for Azra or Charity, I confess I never had the pleasure of meeting her in polite society'.

But despite his colourful private life, "polite society" did come to recognise his literary talents, and in the New Year Honours List for 1838 he was awarded a baronetcy for his services to literature.

The Haunted and the Haunters, the last tale in this collection, appeared anonymously in *Blackwoods* in 1859. It appears to be based on Bulwer's experiments with the popular American spiritualist Daniel Dunglas Home. In his constant pursuit of the science of metaphysics, Bulwer was intrigued by Home's seances and after witnessing a performance wrote to his son about Home's ability to summon spirits declaring, 'it is very curious, and if there be a trick it is hard to conceive it'. Home's second wife recorded many of the happenings witnessed by Bulwer and her husband during their meetings at Bulwer's homes in Ealing and Knebworth. She always cherished a deep resentment of Bulwer for never giving them his public support[1]. 'In public he was an investigator of spiritualism, in private a believer,' she declared. But Bulwer's views, as expressed in the conclusion to *The Haunted and the Haunters,* do not discount belief: 'The Supernatural is the impossible and that which is called supernatural is only a something in the laws of nature of which we have hitherto been ignorant.'

In its original form, *The Haunted and the Haunters* was longer than the version printed here, but Bulwer cut the extra chapter when the tale was reprinted, using its theme, immortality, as the basis of *A Strange Story* (1861) which Dickens persuaded Bulwer to write as a serial for his magazine *All The Year Round.* The shortened version has become the standard.

---

[1] On one occasion she recorded that: 'Sir Edward felt himself gently touched on the knee, and on putting down his hand a cross was placed on it.' The cross 'which was of cardboard had been lying with some other articles on a table at the end of a large room'.

Through his career, at various stages, Bulwer wrote historical novels, novels of contemporary life, crime or *Newgate* novels, but from *Narenor* in 1824 to *The Coming Race* in 1871, his fantasy and supernatural work never ceased. Those who believed, like W. E. Aytoun, that he wrote on the occult purely for financial reasons are mistaken. Rather, he genuinely sought spiritual knowledge and through his research, study and resulting fiction sought to identify, 'those subtle recesses in the ethics of human life in which Truth and Falsehood dwell undisturbed and unseparated.'

William Lawrence
February 2000

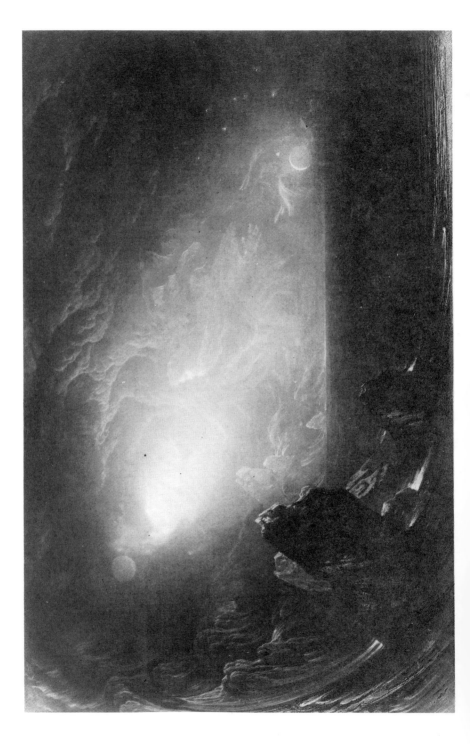

A MANUSCRIPT FOUND IN A MADHOUSE

I am the eldest son of a numerous family,—noble in birth, and eminent for wealth. My brothers are a vigorous and comely race,—my sisters are more beautiful than dreams. By what fatality was it that I alone was thrust into this glorious world distorted, and dwarf-like, and hideous,—my limbs a mockery, my countenance a horror, myself a blackness on the surface of creation,—a discord in the harmony of nature, a living misery, an animated curse? I am shut out from the aims and objects of my race;—with the deepest sources of affection in my heart, I am doomed to find no living thing on which to pour them. Love!—out upon the word—I am its very loathing and abhorrence: friendship turns from me in disgust; pity beholds me, and withers to aversion. Wheresoever I wander, I am encompassed with hatred as with an atmosphere. Whatever I attempt, I am in the impassable circle of a dreadful and accursed doom. Ambition—pleasure—philanthropy—fame—the common blessing of social intercourse—are all as *other* circles, which *mine* can touch but in *one* point, and that point is torture. I have knowledge to which the wisdom of ordinary sages is as dust to gold;—I have energies to which relaxation is pain;—I have benevolence which sheds itself in charity and love over a worm! For what—merciful God!—for what are these blessings of nature or of learning?—The instant I employ them, I must enter among men: the moment I enter among men, my being blackens into an agony. Laughter grins upon me—terror dogs my steps;—I exist upon poisons, and my nourishment is scorn!

At my birth the nurse refused me suck; my mother saw me and became delirious; my father ordered that I should be stifled as a monster. The physicians saved my life—accursed be they for the act! One woman—she was old and childless—took compassion upon me; she reared and fed me. I grew up—I asked for something to love; I loved every thing; the common earth—the fresh grass—the living insect—the household brute;—from the dead stone I trod on, to the sublime countenance of man, made to behold the stars and to scorn *me*;—from the noblest thing to the prettiest—the fairest to the foulest—I loved them *all!* I knelt to my mother, and besought her to love me—she shuddered. I fled to my father,—and he spurned me! The lowest minion of the human race that had its limbs shapen and its countenance formed, refused to consort with me;—the very dog (I only dared to seek out one that seemed more rugged and hideous than its fellows), the very dog dreaded me, and slunk away! I grew up lonely and wretched; I was like the reptile whose prison is the stone's heart,—immured in the eternal penthouse of a solitude to which the breath of fellowship never came;—girded with a wall of barrenness, and flint, and doomed to vegetate and batten on my own suffocating and poisoned meditations. But while this was my *heart's* dungeon, they could not take from the *external* senses the sweet face of the Universal Nature;—they could not bar me from commune with the voices of the mighty Dead. Earth opened to me her marvels, and the volumes of the wise their stores. I read—I mused—I examined—I descended into the deep wells of Truth—and mirrored in my soul the holiness of her divine beauty. The past lay before me like a scroll; the mysteries of this breathing world rose from the present like clouds;—even of the dark future, experience shadowed forth something of a token and a sign; and over the wonders of the world, I hung the intoxicating and mingled spells of poesy and of knowledge. But I could not without a struggle live in a world of love, and be the only thing doomed to hatred. "I will travel," said I, "to other quarters of the globe. All earth's tribes have not the proud stamp of angels and of gods, and amongst its infinite variety I may find a being who will not sicken at myself." I took leave of the only one who had not loathed me—the women who had given me food, and reared me up to life. She had now become imbecile, and doting, and blind;—so she did not disdain to lay her hand upon my distorted head, and to bless me. "But better," she said, even as she blessed me and in despite of her dotage,—"better that you had perished in the womb!" And I laughed with a loud laugh when I heard her, and rushed from the house.

One evening, in my wanderings, as I issued from a wood, I came abruptly upon the house of a village priest. Around it, from a thick and lofty fence of shrubs which the twilight of summer bathed in dew, the honeysuckle, and the sweetbrier, and the wild rose sent forth those gifts of fragrance and delight which were not denied even unto me. As I walked slowly behind the hedge, I heard voices on the opposite side; they were the voices of women, and I paused to listen. They spoke of love, and of the qualities which should create it.

18

"No," said one, and the words, couched in a tone of music, thrilled to my heart,—"no, it is not beauty which I require in a lover; it is the mind which can command others, and the passion which would bow that mind unto me. I ask for genius and affection. I ask for nothing else."

"But," said the other voice, "you could not love a monster in person, even if he were a miracle of intellect and of love!"

"I could," answered the first speaker, fervently; "if I know my own heart, I could. You remember the fable of a girl whom a monster loved! I could have loved *that* monster."

And with these words they passed from my hearing; but I stole round, and through a small crevice in the fence, beheld the face and form of the speaker, whose words had opened, as it were, a glimpse of Heaven to my heart. Her eyes were soft, and deep,—her hair parting from her girlish, and smooth brow, was of the hue of gold,—her aspect was pensive and melancholy,—and over the delicate and transparent paleness of her cheek, hung the wanness, but also the eloquence of thought. To other eyes she might not have been beautiful,—to mine, her face was as an angel's.—Oh! lovelier far than the visions of the Carian, or the shapes that floated before the eyes of the daughters of Delos, is the countenance of one that bringeth to the dark breast the first glimmerings of Hope! From that hour my resolution was taken: I concealed myself in the wood that bordered her house; I made my home with the wild fox in the cavern, and the shade; the day-light passed in dreams, and passionate delirium,—and at evening I wandered forth, to watch afar off her footstep; or creep through the copse, unseen, to listen to her voice; or through the long and lone night to lie beneath the shadow of the house, and fix my soul, watchful as a star, upon the windows of the chamber where she slept. I strewed her walks with the leaves of poetry, and at midnight I made the air audible with the breath of music. In my writings and my songs, whatever in the smooth accents of praise, or the burning language of passion, or the liquid melodies of verse, could awaken her fancy or excite her interest, I attempted. Curses on the attempt! May the hand wither!—may the brain burn! May the heart shrivel, and parch like a leaf that a flame devours—from which the cravings of my ghastly and unnatural love found a channel, or an aid! I told her in my verses, in my letters, that I had overheard her confession. I told her that I was more hideous than the demons which the imagination of a Northern savage had ever bodied forth;—I told her that I was a thing which the day-light loathed to look upon;—but I told her also, that I adored her: and I breathed both my story and my love in the numbers of song, and sung them to the silver chords of my lute, with a voice which belied my form, and was not out of harmony with nature. She answered me,—and her answer filled the air, that had hitherto been to me a breathing torture, with enchantment and rapture. She repeated, that beauty was as nothing in her estimation—that to her all loveliness was in the soul. She told me that one who wrote as I wrote—who felt as I felt—could not be loathsome in her eyes. She told me that she could love me, be my form even more monstrous than I had portrayed it. Fool!—miserable fool that I was, to believe her! So then, shrouded among the trees, and wrapped from head to foot in a mantle, and safe in the oath by which I had bound her not to seek to penetrate my secret, or to behold my form before the hour I myself should appoint, arrived—I held commune with her in the deep nights of summer, and beneath the unconscious stars; and while I unrolled to her earnest spirit the marvels of the mystic world, and the glories of wisdom, I mingled with my instruction the pathos and the passion of love!

"Go," said she one night as we conferred together, and through the matted trees I saw—though she beheld me not—that her cheek blushed as she spoke; "Go,—and win from others the wonder that you have won from me. Go,—pour forth your knowledge to the crowd; go, gain the glory of fame—the glory which makes man immortal—and then come back, and claim me,—I will be yours!"

"Swear it!" cried I.

"I swear!" she said; and as she spoke the moonlight streamed upon her face, flushed as it was with the ardour of the moment and the strangeness of the scene; her eye burnt with a steady and deep fire—her lip was firm—and her figure, round which the light fell like the glory of a halo, seemed instinct and swelling, as it were, with the determinate energy of the soul. I gazed—and my heart leapt within me;—I answered not—but I stole silently away: for months she heard of me no more.

I fled to a lonely and far spot,—I surrounded myself once more with books. I explored once more the arcana of science; I ransacked once more the starry regions of poetry; and then upon the mute page I poured the thoughts and the treasures which I had stored within me! I sent the product, without a name, upon the world: the world received it; approved it; and it became fame.

Philosophers bowed in wonder before my discoveries; the pale student in cell and cloister, pored over the mines of learning which I had dragged into day; the maidens in their bowers blushed and sighed, as they drank in the burning pathos of my verse. The old and the young,—all sects and all countries, united in applause and enthusiasm for the unknown being who held, as they averred, the Genii of wisdom and the Spirits of verse in mighty and wizard spells, which few had ever won, and none had ever blended before.

I returned to *her*,—I sought a meeting under the same mystery and conditions as of old,—I proved myself that unknown whose fame filled all ears, and occupied all tongues. Her heart had foreboded it already! I claimed my reward! And in the depth and deadness of night, when not a star crept through the curtain of cloud and gloom—when not a gleam struggled against the blackness—not a breath stirred the heavy torpor around us—that reward was yielded. The dense woods and the eternal hills were the sole witness of our bridals;—and girt with darkness as with a robe, she leant upon my bosom, and shuddered not at the place of her repose!

Thus only we met;—but for months we *did* meet, and I was blessed. At last, the fruit of our ominous love could no longer be concealed. It became necessary, either that I should fly with her, or wed her with the rites and ceremonies of man—as I had done amidst the more sacred solemnities of nature. In either case, disclosure was imperious and unavoidable;—I took therefore that which gratitude ordained. Beguiled by her assurances—touched by her trust, and tenderness—maddened by her tears—duped by my own heart—I agreed to meet her, and for the first time openly reveal myself—at the foot of the altar!

The appointed day came. At our mutual wish, only two witnesses were present, beside the priest and the aged and broken-hearted father, who consented solely to our singular marriage because mystery was less terrible to him than disgrace. *She* had prepared them to see a distorted and fearful abortion,—but—ha! ha! ha!—she had not prepared them to see *me!* I entered:—all eyes, but *her's*, were turned to me,—an unanimous cry was uttered—the priest involuntarily closed the book, and muttered the exorcism for a fiend—the father covered his face with his hands, and sunk upon the ground—the other witnesses—ha! ha! ha! (it was rare mirth!)—rushed screaming from the chapel. It was twilight—the tapers burned dim and faint—I approached my bride—who, trembling and weeping beneath her long veil, had not dared to look at me. "Behold me!"—said I—"my bride, my beloved!—behold thy husband!"—I raised her veil—she saw my countenance glare full upon her—uttered one shriek, and fell senseless on the floor. I raised her not—I stirred not—I spoke not. I saw my doom was fixed, my curse complete; and my heart lay mute, and cold, and dead within me, like a stone! Others entered, they bore away the bride. By little and little, the crowd assembled, to gaze upon the monster in mingled derision and dread;—*then* I recollected myself and arose. I scattered them in terror before me,—and uttering a single and piercing cry, I rushed forth, and hid myself in the wood.

But at night, at the hour in which I had been accustomed to meet her, I stole forth again. I approached the house, I climbed the wall, I entered the window; I was in her chamber. All was still and solitary; I saw not a living thing there; but the lights burned bright and clear. I drew near to the bed; I beheld a figure stretched upon it—a taper at the feet, and a taper at the head,—so there was plenty of light for me to see my bride. She was a corpse! I did not speak—nor faint—nor groan;—but I laughed aloud. Verily it is a glorious mirth, to behold the only thing one loves stiff, and white, and shrunken, and food for the red, playful, creeping worm! I raised my eyes, and saw upon a table near the bed, something covered with a black cloth. I lifted the cloth, and beheld—ha! ha! ha!—by the foul fiend!—a dead—but beautiful likeness of myself! A little infant monster! The ghastly mouth, and the laidly features—the delicate, green, corpse-like hue—and the black shaggy hair—and the horrible limbs, and the unnatural shape—there—ha! ha!—there they were—my wife and my child! I took them both in my arms—I hurried from the house—I carried them into the wood. I concealed them in a cavern—I watched over them—and lay beside them,—and played with the worms—that played with them—ha! ha! ha!—it was a jovial time that, in the old cavern!

And so then they were all gone but the bones, I buried them quietly, and took my way to my home. My father was dead, and my brothers hoped that I was dead also. But I turned them out of the house, and took possession of the titles and the wealth. And then I went to see the doting woman who had nursed me; and they shewed me where she slept—a little green mound in the church-yard—and I wept—Oh, so bitterly! I never shed a tear for my wife—or—ha! ha! ha!—for my beautiful child!

And so I lived *happily* enough for a short time; but at last they discovered that I was the unknown philosopher—the divine poet whom the world rung of. And the crowd came—and the mob beset me—and my rooms were filled with eyes—large, staring eyes, all surveying me from head to foot—and peals of laughter and shrieks wandered about the air, like disembodied and damned spirits— and I was never alone again!

MONOS AND DAIMONOS
A Legend

I am English by birth, but my early years were passed in a foreign and more northern land. I had neither brothers nor sisters; my mother died when I was in the cradle; and I found my sole companion, tutor, and playmate in my father. He was a younger brother of a noble and ancient house: what induced him to forsake his country and his friends, to abjure all society, and to live on a rock is a story in itself, which has nothing to do with mine.

I said my father lived on a rock—the whole country round seemed nothing but rock!—wastes, bleak, blank, dreary; trees stunted, herbage blighted; caverns, through which some black and wild stream (that never knew star or sunlight, but through rare and hideous chasms of the huge stones above it) went dashing and howling on its blessed course; vast cliffs, covered with eternal snows, where the birds of prey lived, and sent, in screams and discordance, a grateful and meet music to the heavens, which seemed too cold and barren to wear even clouds upon their wan, grey comfortless expanse: these made the character of that country where the spring of my life sickened itself away. The climate which, in the milder parts of * * * *, relieves the nine months of winter with three months of an abrupt and autumnless summer, never seemed to vary in the gentle and sweet region in which *my* home was placed. Perhaps, for a brief interval, the snow in the valleys melted, and the streams swelled, and a blue, ghastly, unnatural kind of vegetation, seemed here and there to scatter a grim smile over minute particles of the universal rock; but to these witnesses of the changing season were the summers of my boyhood confined. My father was addicted to the sciences—the physical sciences—and possessed but a moderate share of learning in anything else; he taught me all he knew; and the rest of my education, Nature, in a savage and stern guise, instilled into my heart by silent but deep lessons. She taught my feet to bound, and my arm to smite; she breathed life into my passions, and shed darkness over my temper; she taught me to cling to her, even in her most rugged and unalluring form, and to shrink from all else— from the companionship of man, and the soft smiles of woman, and the shrill voice of childhood; and the ties, and hopes, and social gaieties of existence, as from a torture and a curse. Even in that sullen rock, and beneath that ungenial sky, I had luxuries unknown to the palled tastes of cities, or to those who woo delight in an air of odours and in a land of roses! What were those luxuries? They had a myriad varieties and shades of enjoyment—they had but a common name. What were those luxuries?—*Solitude!*

My father died when I was eighteen; I was transferred to my uncle's protection, and I repaired to London. I arrived there, gaunt and stern, a giant in limbs and strength, and, to the judgment of those about me, a savage in mood and bearing. They would have laughed, but I awed them; they would have altered *me*, but I changed *them*; I threw a damp over their enjoyments. Though I said little, though I sat with them estranged, and silent, and passive, they seemed to wither beneath my presence. Nobody could live with me and be happy, or at ease! I felt it, and I hated them that they could not love me. Three years passed—I was of age—I demanded my fortune—and scorning social life, and pining once more for loneliness, I resolved to journey to those unpeopled and far lands, which if any have pierced, none have returned to describe. So I took my leave of them all, cousin and aunt—and when I came to my old uncle, who had loved me less than any, I grasped his hand with so friendly a gripe, that, well I ween, the dainty and nice member was thenceforth but little inclined to its ordinary functions.

I commenced my pilgrimage—I pierced the burning sands—I traversed the vast deserts—I came into the enormous woods of Africa, where human step never trod, nor human voice ever startled the thrilling and intense solemnity that broods over the great solitudes, as it brooded over chaos before the world was! There the primeval nature springs and perishes, undisturbed and unvaried by the convulsions of the surrounding world; the seed becomes the tree, lives through its uncounted ages, falls and moulders, and rots and vanishes: there the slow Time moves on, unwitnessed in its mighty and mute changes, save by the wandering lion, or that huge serpent—a hundred times more vast than the puny boa—which travellers have boasted to behold. There, too, as beneath the heavy and dense shade I couched in the scorching noon, I heard the trampling as of an army, and the crush and fall of the strong trees, and saw through the matted boughs the Behemoth pass on its terrible way, with its eyes burning as a sun, and its white teeth arched and glistening in the rabid jaw, as pillars of spar glitter in a cavern: the monster, to whom those wastes only are a home, and who never, since the waters rolled from the Dædal earth, has been given to human gaze and wonder but my own! Seasons glided on, but I counted them not; they were not doled to me by the tokens of man, nor made sick to me by the changes of his base life, and the evidence of his sordid labour. Seasons glided on, and my youth ripened into manhood, and manhood grew grey with the first frost of age; and then a vague and restless spirit fell upon me, and I said in my foolish heart, "I will look upon the countenances of my race once more!" I retraced my steps—I re-crossed the wastes—I re-entered the cities—I resumed the garb of man; for I had been hitherto naked in the wilderness, and hair had grown over me as a garment. I repaired to a seaport, and took ship for England.

In the vessel there was one man, and only one, who neither avoided my companionship nor recoiled at my frown. He was an idle and curious being, full of the frivolities, and egotisms, and importance of those to whom towns are homes and talk has become a mental aliment. He was one pervading, irritating, offensive tissue of little and low thoughts. The only meanness he had not was fear. It was impossible to awe, to silence, or to shun him. He sought me for ever; he was as a blister to me, which no force could tear away; my soul grew faint when my eyes met him. He was to my sight as those creatures which, from their very loathsomeness, are fearful as well as despicable to us. I longed and yearned to strangle him when he addressed me! Often I would have laid my hand on him, and hurled him into the sea to the sharks, which lynx-eyed and eager-jawed, swam night and day around our ship; but the gaze of many was on us, and I curbed myself, and turned away, and shut my eyes in very sickness; and when I opened them again, lo! he was by my side, and his sharp quick voice grated on my loathing ear! One night I was roused from my sleep by the screams and oaths of men, and I hastened on deck: we had struck upon a rock. It was a ghastly, but a glorious sight! Moonlight still and calm —the sea sleeping in sapphires; and in the midst of the silent and soft repose of all things, three hundred and fifty souls were to perish from the world! I sat apart, and looked on, and aided not. A voice crept like an adder's hiss into my ear; I turned, and saw my tormentor; the moonlight fell on his face, and it grinned with the maudlin grin of intoxication, and his pale blue eye glistened, and he said, "We will not part even here!" My blood ran coldly through my veins, and I would have thrown him into the sea, which now came fast and fast upon us; but the moonlight was on him, and I did not dare to kill him. But I would not stay to perish with the herd, and I threw myself alone from the vessel and swam towards a rock. I saw a shark dart after me, but I shunned him, and the moment after he had plenty to sate his maw. I heard a crash, and a mingled and wild burst of anguish,—the anguish of three hundred and fifty hearts that a minute afterwards were stilled, and I said to my own heart, with a deep joy, "*His* voice is with the rest, and we *have* parted!" I gained the shore, and lay down to sleep.

The next morning my eyes opened upon a land more beautiful than a young man's dreams. The sun had just risen, and laughed over streams of silver, and trees bending with golden and purple fruits, and the diamond dew sparkled from a sod covered with flowers, whose faintest breath was a delight. Ten thousand birds, with all the hues of a northern rainbow blended in their glorious and glowing wings, rose from turf and tree, and loaded the air with melody and gladness; the sea, without a vestige of the past destruction upon its glassy brow, murmured at my feet; the heavens, without a cloud, and bathed in a liquid and radiant light, sent their breezes as a blessing to my cheek. I rose with a refreshed and light heart; I traversed the new home I had found: I climbed a hill, and saw that I was in a small island; it had no trace of man, and my heart swelled as I gazed around and cried aloud in my exultation, "I shall be alone again!" I descended the hill: I had not yet reached its foot, when I saw the figure of a man approaching towards me. I looked at him, and my heart misgave me. He drew nearer, and I saw that my despicable persecutor had escaped the waters, and now stood before me. He came up with his hideous grin and his twinkling eye; and he flung his arms round me—I would sooner have felt the slimy folds of the serpent—and said, with his grating and harsh voice, "Ha! ha! my friend, we shall be together still!" I looked at him with a grim brow, but I said not a word. There was a great cave by the shore, and I walked down and entered it, and the man followed me. "We shall live so happily here," said he; "we will never separate!" And my lip trembled, and my hand clenched of its own accord. It was now noon, and hunger came upon me; I went forth and killed a deer, and I brought it home and broiled part of it on a fire of fragrant wood; and the man ate, and crunched, and laughed, and I wished that the bones had choked him; and he said, when we had done, "We shall have rare cheer here!" But I still held my peace. At last he stretched himself in a corner of the cave and slept. I looked at him, and saw that the slumber was heavy; and I went out and rolled a huge stone to the mouth of the cavern, and took my way to the opposite part of the island;—it was my turn to laugh then! I found out another cavern; and I made a bed of moss and of leaves, and I wrought a table of wood, and I looked out from the mouth of the cavern and saw the wide seas before me, and I said, "Now I shall be alone!"

When the next day came, I again went out and caught a kid, and brought it in, and prepared it as before; but I was not hungered and I could not eat, so I roamed forth and returned. I entered the cavern, and sitting on my bed and by my table was that man whom I thought I had left buried alive in the other cave. He laughed when he saw me, and laid down the bone he was gnawing.

"Ha, ha!" said he, "you would have served me a rare trick; but there was a hole in the cave which you did not see, and I got out to seek you. It was not a difficult matter, for the island is so small; and now we *have* met, and we will part no more!"

I said to the man, "Rise and follow me!" So he rose, and the food he quitted was loathsome in my eyes, for he had touched it. "Shall this thing reap and sow?" thought I; and my heart felt to me like iron.

I ascended a tall cliff. "Look round," said I; "you see that stream which divides the island, you shall dwell on one side, and I on the other: but the same spot shall not hold us, nor the same feast supply!"

"That may never be!" quoth the man; "for I cannot catch the deer, nor spring upon the mountain kid; and if you feed me not I shall starve!"

"Are there not fruits," said I, "and birds that you may snare, and fishes which the sea throws up?"

"But I like them not," quoth the man, and laughed, "so well as the flesh of kids and deer!"

"Look, then," said I, "look! by that grey stone, upon the opposite side of the stream, I will lay a deer or a kid daily, so that you may have the food you covet; but if ever you cross the stream and come into my kingdom, so sure as the sea murmurs, and the bird flies, I will slay you!"

I descended the cliff, and led the man to the side of the stream. "I cannot swim," said he; so I took him on my shoulders and crossed the brook, and I found him out a cave, and I made him a bed and a table like my own, and left him. When I was on my own side of the stream again, I bounded with joy, and lifted up my voice; "I shall be alone *now*!" said I.

So two days passed, and I *was* alone. On the third I went after my prey; the noon was hot, and I was wearied when I returned. I entered my cavern, and, behold, the man lay stretched upon my bed. "Ha, ha!" said he, "here I am; I was so lonely at home that I have come to live with you again!"

I frowned on the man with a dark brow, and I said, "So sure as the sea murmurs, and the bird flies, I will slay you!" I seized him in my arms; plucked him from my bed; I took him out into the open air, and we stood together on the smooth sand and by the great sea. A fear came suddenly upon me: I was struck with the awe of the still Spirit which reigns over Solitude. Had a thousand been round us, I would have slain him before them all. I feared now because we were alone in the desert, with Silence and GOD! I relaxed my hold. "Swear," I said, "never to molest me again; swear to preserve unpassed the boundary of our several homes, and I will *not* kill you!" "I cannot swear," answered the man, "I would sooner die than forswear the blessed human face,—even though that face be my enemy's!"

At these words my rage returned; I dashed the man to the ground, and I put my foot upon his breast, and my hand upon his neck, and he struggled for a moment—and was dead! I was startled; and as I looked upon his face I thought he seemed to revive; I thought the cold blue eye fixed upon me, and the vile grin returned to the livid mouth, and the hands which in the death-pang had grasped the sand, stretched themselves out to me. So I stamped on the breast again, and I dug a hole in the shore, and I buried the body. "And now," said I, "I am alone at last!" And then *the* TRUE *sense of loneliness,* the vague, comfortless, objectless sense of desolation passed into me. And I shook—shook in every limb of my giant frame, as if I had been a child that trembles in the dark; and my hair rose, and my flesh crept, and I would not have stayed in that spot a moment more if I had been made young again for it. I turned away and fled—fled round the whole island; and gnashed my teeth when I came to the sea, and longed to be cast into some illimitable desert, that I might flee on for ever. At sunset I returned to my cave; I sat myself down on one corner of the bed, and covered my face with my hands; I thought I heard a noise; I raised my eyes, and , as I live, I saw on the other end of the bed the man whom I had slain and buried. There he sat, six feet from me, and nodded to me, and looked at me with his wan eyes, and laughed. I rushed from the cave—I entered a wood—I threw myself down—there, opposite to me, six feet from my face, was the face of that man again! And my courage rose, and I spoke, but he answered not. I attempted to seize him, he glided from my grasp, and was still opposite, six feet from me as before. I flung myself on the ground, and pressed my face to the sod, and would not look up till the night came on, and darkness was over the earth. I then rose and returned to the cave; I lay down on my bed, and the man lay down by me; and I frowned, and tried to seize him as before, but I could not, and I closed my eyes, *and the man lay by me.* Day followed day and it was the same. At board, at bed, at home and abroad, in my uprising and my downsitting, by day and at night,—there, by my bedside, six feet from me, and no more, was that ghastly and dead thing. And I said, as I looked upon the beautiful land and the still heavens, and then turned to that fearful comrade, "I shall never be alone again!" And the man laughed.

At last a ship came, and I hailed it; it took me up, and I thought, as I put my foot upon the deck, "I shall escape from my tormentor!" As I thought so, I saw him climb the deck too, and I strove to push him down into the sea, but in vain; he was by my side, *and he fed and slept with me as before*! I came home to my native land. I forced myself into crowds—I went to the feast, and I heard music; and I made thirty men sit with me, and watch by day and by night. So I had thirty-*one* companions, and one was more social than all the rest.

At last I said to myself, "This is a delusion, and a cheat of the external senses, and the thing is *not*, save in my mind. I will consult those skilled in such disorders, and I will be—*alone again!*"

I summoned one celebrated in purging from the mind's eye its qualms and deceits—I bound him by an oath to secrecy—and I told him my tale. He was a bold man and a learned, and promised me relief and release.

"Where is the figure now?" said he, smiling; "I see it not."

And I answered, "It is six feet from us!"

"I see it not," said he again; "and if it were real, my senses would not receive the image less palpably than yours." And he spoke to me as schoolmen speak. I did not argue nor reply, but I

31

ordered the servants to prepare a room, and to cover the floor with a thick layer of sand. When it was done, I bade the leech follow me into the room, and I barred the door. "Where is the figure now?" repeated he: and I said, "Six feet from us as before!" And the leech smiled. "Look on the floor!" said I, and pointed to the spot; "what see you?" and the leech shuddered, and clung to me that he might not fall. "The sand there," said he, "was smooth when we entered; and now I see on that spot the print of human feet!"

And I laughed, and dragged my *living* companion on. "See," said I, "where we move what follows us!"

The leech gasped for breath: "The print," said he, "of those human feet!"

"Can you not minister to me then?" cried I, in a sudden and fierce agony; "and must I *never* be alone again?"

And I saw the feet of the dead thing trace these words upon the sand:—

"SOLITUDE IS ONLY FOR THE GUILTLESS—EVIL THOUGHTS ARE COMPANIONS FOR A TIME—EVIL DEEDS ARE COMPANIONS THROUGH ETERNITY—THY HATRED MADE ME BREAK UPON THY LONELINESS—THY CRIME DESTROYS LONELINESS FOR EVER!"

THE NYMPH OF THE LURLEI BERG — A Tale

O Syrens, beware of a fair young Knight,
He loves and he rides away *

A group of armed men were sitting cheerlessly round a naked and ill-furnished board in one of those rugged castles that overhang the Rhine—they looked at the empty bowl, and they looked at the untempting platter—then they shrugged their shoulders, and looked foolishly at each other. A young Knight, of a better presence than the rest, stalked gloomily into the hall.

"Well, comrades," said he, pausing in the centre of the room, and leaning on his sword, " I grieve to entertain ye no better—my father's gold is long gone—it bought your services while it lasted, and with these services, I Rupert the Fearnought, won this castle from its Lord—levied tools on the river—plundered the Burgesses of Bingen—and played the chieftain as nobly as a robber may. But alas! wealth flies—luck deserts us—we can no longer extract a doit from traveller or citizen. We must separate."

The armed men muttered something unintelligible—then they looked again at the dishes—then they shook their heads very dismally, and Rupert the Fearnought continued—

"For my part I love every thing wealth purchases—I cannot live in poverty, and when you have all gone, I propose to drown myself in the Rhine."

The armed men shouted out very noisily their notions on the folly of such a project of relief, but Rupert sunk on a stone seat, folded his arms, and scarcely listened to them.

"Ah, if one could get some of the wealth that lies in the Rhine!" said an old marauder, " that would be worth diving for!"

"There cannot be much gold among the fishes I fancy," growled out another marauder, as he played with his dagger.

"Thou art a fool," quoth the old man; "gold there is, for I heard my father say so, and it may be won too by a handsome man, if he be brave enough."

Rupert lifted his head—"And how?" said he.

"The Water Spirits have the key to the treasure, and he who wins their love, may perhaps win their gold."

Rupert rose and took the old robber aside; they conversed

34

long and secretly, and Rupert, returning to the hall, called for the last hogshead of wine the cellar contained.

"Comrades," said he, as he quaffed off a bumper, "Comrades, pledge to my safe return; I shall leave ye for a single month, since one element can yield no more, to try the beings of another; I may perish—I may return not. Tarry for me, therefore, but the time I have mentioned; if ye then see me not, depart in peace. Meanwhile, ye may manage to starve on, and if the worst come to the worst, ye can eat one another."

So saying, the young spendthrift (by birth a Knight, by necessity a Robber, and by name and nature, Rupert the Fearnought) threw down the cup, and walking forth from the hall, left his companions to digest his last words with what appetite they might.

Among the Spirits of the Water, none were like Lurline, she was gentle as the gentlest breeze that floats from the realms of Spring over the bosom of the Rhine, and wherever at night she glided along the waves, there the beams of the love-star lingered, and lit up her path with their tenderest ray. Her eyes were of the softest azure of a southern heaven, and her hair like its setting sun. But above all her charms was the melody of her voice, and often when she sat upon the Lurlei Rock by the lonely moonlight, and sent her wild song above the silent waters, the nightingale paused from her wail to listen, and the winds crept humbled round her feet, as at a Sorcerer's spell.

One night as she thus sat, and poured forth her charmed strains, she saw a boat put from the opposite shore, and as it approached nearer and nearer towards her, she perceived it was guided by one solitary mariner; the moonlight rested upon his upward face, and it was the face of manhood's first dawn—beautiful, yet stern, and daring in its beauty—the light curls, surmounted by a plumed semi-casque, danced above a brow that was already marked by thought; and something keen and proud in the mien and air of the stranger, designated one who had learnt to act no less than to meditate. The Water Spirit paused as he approached and gazed admiringly upon the fairest form that had ever yet chanced upon her solitude; she noted that the stranger too kept his eyes fixed upon her, and steered his boat to the rock on which she sat. And the shoals then as now were fraught with danger, but she laid her spell upon the wave and upon the rock, and the boat glided securely over them,—and the bold stranger was within but a few paces of her seat, when she forbade the waters to admit his nearer approach. The stranger stood erect in the boat, as it rocked tremulously to and fro, and still gazing upon the Water Nymph, he said—

"Who art thou, O beautiful maiden! and whence is thine art? Night after night I have kept watch among the wild rocks that tenanted the sacred Goar, and listened enamoured to thy lay. Never before on earth was such minstrelsy heard. Art thou a daughter of the river? and dost thou—as the greybeards say—lure us to destruction? Behold I render myself up to thee! Sweet is Death if it cradle me in thine arms! Welcome the whirlpool, if it entomb me in thy home!"

"Thou art bold, young mortal"—said the Water Spirit, with trembling tones, for she felt already the power of Love. "And wherefore say thy tribe such harsh legends of my song? Who ever perished by my art? Return to thine home safely and in peace, and vindicate, when thou hearest it maligned, the name of the Water Spirit of the Rhine."

"Return!"—said the Stranger haughtily—"never, until I have touched thee—knelt to thee—felt that thy beauty is not a dream. Even now my heart bounds as I gaze on thee! Even now I feel that thou *shalt* be mine! Behold! I trust myself to thine element! I fear nothing but the loss of thee!"

So saying the young man leapt into the water, and in a minute more he knelt by the side of Lurline.

It was the stillest hour of night; the stars were motionless in the heavens: the moonlight lay hushed on the rippling tide:—from cliff to vale, no living thing was visible, save them, the Spirit and her human wooer.

"Oh!"—said he, passionately,—"never did I believe that thy voice was aught but some bodily music from another world; in madness, and without hope, I tracked its sound homeward, and I have found *thee*. I touch thee!—thou livest!—the blood flows in thy form!—thou art as woman, but more lovely! Take me to thy blue caverns and be my bride!"

As a dream from the sleeper, as a vapour from the valley, Lurline glided from the arms of the stranger, and sunk into the waters; the wave closed over her, but, beneath its surface, he saw, and plunged into the waves!

The morning came, and the boat still tossed by the Lurlei

Berg—without a hand to steer it. The Rhine rolled bright to the dewy sun, but the stranger had returned not to its shores.

The cavern of the Water Spirit stretches in many chambers beneath the courses of the river, and in its inmost recess—several days after the stranger's disappearance—Lurline sat during the summer noon; but not alone. Love lighted up those everlasting spars, and even beneath the waters and beneath the earth held his temple and his throne.

"And tell me, my stranger Bridegroom,"—said Lurline, as the stranger lay at her feet, listening to the dash of the waters against the cavern—"tell me of what country and parentage art thou? Art thou one of the many chiefs whose castles frown from the opposite cliffs?—or a wanderer from some distant land? What is thy mortal name?"

"Men call me Rupert the Fearnought,"—answered the stranger. "A penniless chief am I, and a cheerless castle do I hold; my sword is my heritage;—and as for gold, the gold which my Sire bequeathed me, alas! on the land, beautiful Lurline, there are many more ways of getting rid of such dross than in thy peaceful dominions beneath the river. Yet, Lurline"—and the countenance of Rupert became more anxious and more earnest—"Is it not true that the Spirits of thy race hoard vast treasures of gems and buried gold within their caves? Do ye not gather all that the wind and tempest have sunk beneath the waves in your rocky coffers? And have ye not the power to endow a mortal with the forgotten wealth of ages?"

"Ah, yes!"—answered the enamoured Water Spirit. "These chambers contain enough of such idle treasures, dull and useless, my beloved, to those who love."

"Eh—em!"—quoth the mortal—"what thou sayest has certainly a great deal of truth in it; but—but just to pass away the next hour or two—suppose thou showest me, dearest Lurline, some of these curiosities of thine. Certes[1] I am childishly fond of looking at coins and jewels."

"As thou wilt, my stranger," answered Lurline, and, rising, she led the way through the basalt arches that swept in long defiles through her palace, singing with the light heart of contented love to the waves that dashed around. The stranger followed wondering—but not fearing—with his hand every now and then, as they made some abrupt turning, mechanically wandering to his sword, and his long plume waving lightly to the rushing air, that at times with a hollow roar swept through their mighty prison. At length the Water Spirit came to a door, before which lay an enormous shell, and, as the stranger looked admiringly upon its gigantic size, a monstrous face gradually rose form the aperture of the shell, and with glaring eyes and glistening teeth gloated out upon the mortal.

Three steps backward did Rupert the Fearnought make, and three times did he cross himself with unwonted devotion, and very irreverently, and not in exact keeping with the ceremony, blurted he forth a northern seafarer's oath. Then outflashed his sword; and he asked Lurline if he were to prepare against a foe. The Water Spirit smiled, and murmuring some words in a language unknown to Rupert, the monster slowly wound itself from the cavities of the shell; and, carrying the shell itself upon its back, crept with a long hiss and a trailing slime from the door, circuitously approaching Rupert the Fearnought by the rear. *"Christe beate!"* ejaculated the lover, veering round with extreme celerity, and presenting the point of the sword to the monster. "What singular shell-fish there are at the bottom of the Rhine!" Then, gazing more attentively on the monster, he perceived that it was in the shape of a dragon, substituting only the shell for wings.

"The dragon-race," said the Water Spirit, "are the guardians of all treasure, whether in the water or in the land. And deep in the very centre of the earth, the hugest of the tribe lies coiled around the loadstone of the world."[2]

The door now opened. They entered a vast vault. Heavens! how wondrous was the treasure that greeted the Fearnought's eyes! All the various wrecks that, from the earliest ages of the world, had enriched the Rhine or its tributary streams, contributed their burthen to this mighty treasury! there was the first rude coin ever known in the North, cumbrous and massive, teaching betimes the moral that money is inseparable from the embarrassment of taking care of it. There were Roman vases and jewels in abundance; rings, and chains, and great necklaces of pearl: there, too, were immense fragments of silver that, from time to time, had been washed into the river, and hurried down into this universal recipient. And, looking up, the Fearnought saw that the only roof above was the waters, which rolled black and sullenly overhead, but were prevented either by a magic charm, or the wonderful resistance of the pent air, from penetrating farther. But wild, and loud, and hoarse was the roar above, and the Water Spirit told him, that they were then below the Gewirre or Whirlpool which howls along the bank opposite to the Lurlei Berg.

"I see,"—quoth the bold stranger, as he grasped at a heap of jewels,—"that wherever there is treasure below the surface, there is peril above!"

"Rather say,"—answered the Water Spirit—"that the whirlpool betokens the vexation and strife which are the guardians and parents of riches."

The Fearnought made no answer; but he filled his garments with the most costly gems he could find, in order, doubtless, to examine them more attentively at his leisure.

And that evening as his head lay upon the lap of the Water Spirit, and she played with his wreathy hair, Rupert said, "Ah, Lurline! ah, that thou wouldst accompany me to the land. Thou knowest not in these caves (certainly pretty in their way, but, thou must confess, placed in a prodigiously dull neighbourhood);—thou knowest not, I say, dear Lurline, how charming a life it is to live in a beautiful castle on the land." And with that Rupert began to paint in the most eloquent terms the mode of existence then most approvedly in fashion. He dwelt with a singular flow of words on the pleasures of the chace:[3] he dressed the water-nymph in green—mounted her on a snow-white courser—supposed her the admiration of all who flocked through the green wood to behold her. Then he painted the gorgeous banquet, the Lords and Dames that, glittering in jewels and cloth of gold, would fill the halls over which Lurline should preside—all confessing her beauty, and obedient to her sway; harps were for ever to sound her praises; Minstrels to sing and Knights to contest for it; and, above all, he, Rupert himself, was to be eternally at her feet—"Not, dearest Love," (added he, gently rubbing his knees,) "on these rocky stones, but upon the softest velvets—or, at least, upon the greenest mosses."

The Water Spirit was moved, for the love of change and the dream of Ambition can pierce even below the deepest beds of the stream; and the voice of Flattery is more persuasive than were the melodies of the Syren herself.

By degrees she allowed herself to participate in Rupert's desire for land; and, as she most tenderly loved him, his evident and growing ennui, his long silences, and his frequent yawns, made her anxious to meet his wishes, and fearful lest overwise he should grow utterly wearied of her society. It was settled then that they should go to the land.

"But, oh, my beloved," said Rupert the Fearnought, "I am but a poor and mortgaged Knight, and in my hall the winds whistle through dismantled casements, and over a wineless board. Shall I not go first to the shore, and with some of the baubles thou keepest all uselessly below, refit my castle among yonder vine-clad mountains, so that it shall be a worthy tenement for the Daughter of the Rhine? then I shall hasten back for thee, and we will be wedded with all the pomp that befits thy station."

The poor Water Spirit, having lived at the bottom of the Rhine all her life, was not so well read in the world as might have been expected from a singer of her celebrity. She yielded to the proposition of Rupert; and that very night the moon beheld the beautiful Lurline assisting Rupert to fill his boat (that lay still by the feet of the Lurlei Berg) with all the largest jewels in her treasury. Rupert filled and filled till he began to fear the boat would hold no more without sinking; and then, reluctantly ceasing, he seized the oars, and every now and then kissing his hand at Lurline with a melancholy expression of fondness, he rowed away to the town of St. Goar.

As soon as he had moored his boat in a little creek, overshadowed at that time by thick brambles, he sprang lightly on land; and seizing a hunting-horn that he wore round his neck, sounded a long blast. Five times was that blast echoed from the rock of the Lurlei Berg by the sympathising Dwarf who dwelt there, and who, wiser than Lurline, knew that her mortal lover had parted from her for ever.[4] Rupert started in dismay, but soon recovered his native daring. "Come fiend, sprite, or dragon," said he, "I will not give back the treasure I have won!"

He looked defyingly to the stream, but no shape rose from its depths—the moonlight slept on the water—all was still, and without sign of life, as the echo died mournfully away. He looked wistfully to the land, and now crashing through the boughs came the armed tread of men—plumes waved—corslets glittered, and Rupert the Fearnought was surrounded by his marauding comrades. he stood with one foot on his boat, and pointed exultingly to the treasure. "Behold," he cried, to the old robber who had suggested the coffer of the Spirits of the Deep!"

Then loud broke the robbers' voices over the still stream, and mailed hands grasped the heavy gems, and fierce eyes gloated on their splendour.

"And how didst thou win the treasure?—with thy good sword, we'll warrant," cried the robbers.

"Nay," answered Rupert, "there is a weapon more dangerous to female, whether spirit or flesh, than the sword—a soft tongue and flattering words!—Away; take each what he can carry,—and away, I say, to our castle!"

Days and weeks rolled on, but the Mortal returned not to the Maiden of the Waters; and night after night Lurline sat alone on the moonlight rock, and mourned for her love in such wild and melancholy strains, as now at times the fisherman starts to hear. The Dwarf of the Lurlei Berg sometimes put forth his shagged head, from the little door in his rock, and sought to solace her with wise aphorisms on human inconstancy; but the soft Lurline was not the more consoled by his wisdom, and still not the less she clung to the vain hope that Rupert the Flatterer would return.

And Rupert said to his comrades, as they quaffed the wine, and carved the meat at his castle board—

"I hear there is a maiden in the castle of Lörchausen, amidst the valleys, on the other side the Rhine, fair to see, and rich to wed. She shall be the Bride of the Fearnought."

The robbers shouted at the proposal, and the next day, in their sheenest armour, they accompanied their beautiful chief in his wooing to the Ladye of Lörchausen. But Rupert took care not to cross by the Lurlei Berg; for Fearnought as he was, he thought a defrauded dragon and a betrayed sprite were hard odds for a mortal chief. They arrived at the castle, and Rupert wooed with the same flattery and the same success as before. But as one female generally avenges the wrongs of another, so Rupert was caught by the arts he practised, and loved no less ardently than he was loved. The Chief of Lörchausen consented to the wedding, and the next week he promised to bring the bride and her dowry to the Fearnought's castle.

"But, ah! dearest Unna," said Rupert to his betrothed, "take heed as you pass the river that your bark steer not by the Lurlei Berg, for there lurks a dragon ever athirst for beauty and for gold; and he lashes with his tail the waters when such voyagers as thou pass, and whirls the vessel down into his cave below."

The beautiful Unna was terrified, and promised assent to so reasonable a request.

Rupert and his comrades returned home, and set the old castle in order for the coming of the bride.

The morning broke bright and clear—the birds sang out—the green vines waved merrily on the breeze—and the sunlight danced gaily upon the bosom of the Rhine. Rupert and his comrades stood ranged by the rocky land that borders St. Goar to welcome the bride. And now they heard the trumpets sounding far away, and looking adown the river they saw the feudal streamers of Lörchausen glittering on the tide, as the sail from which they waved cut its way along the waters.

Then the Dwarf of the Lurlei Berg, startled by the noise of the trumpets, peeped peevishly out of his little door, and he saw the vessel on the wave, and Rupert on the land; and at once he knew, as he was a wise dwarf, what was to happen. "Ho, ho!" said he to himself, "not so fast, my young gallant: I have long wanted to marry, myself. What if I get your bride, and what if my good friend the Dragon comfort himself for your fraud by a snap at her dowry—Lurline my cousin shall be avenged!" So with that the dwarf slipped into the water, and running along the cavern, came up to the Dragon quite out of breath. The monster trailed himself hastily out of his shell. "And what now, Master Dwarf," quoth he, very angrily; "no thoroughfare here, I assure you!" "Pooh," said the Dwarf, "are you so stupid that you do not want to be avenged upon the insolent mortal who robbed your treasury, and deserted your mistress. Behold! he stands on the rocks of Goar, about to receive a bride, who sails along with a dowry, that shall swell thy exhausted coffers; behold! I say, I will marry the lady, and thou shalt have the dower."

Then the Dragon was exceedingly pleased—"And how shall it be managed?" said he, rubbing his claws with delight.

"Lock thy door, Master Dragon," answered the Dwarf, "and go up to the Gewirre above thee, and lash the waters with thy tail, so that no boat may approach."

The Dragon promised to obey, and away went Dwarf to Lurline. He found her sitting listlessly in her crystal chamber, her long hair drooping over her face, and her eyes bent on the rocky floor, heavy with tears.

"Arouse thee, cousin," said the Dwarf, "thy lover may be regained. Behold he sails along the Rhine with a bride he is about to marry; and if thou wilt ascend the surface of the water, and sing, with thy sweetest voice, the melodies he loves, doubtless he will not have the heart to resist thee, and thou shalt yet gain the Faithless from his bride."

Lurline started wildly from her seat; she followed the Dwarf up to the Lurlei Berg, and seated herself on a ledge in the rock. The Dwarf pointed out to her in the boat the glittering casque and nodding plumes of the Lord of Löchausen. "Behold thy lover!" said he, "but the helmet hides his face. See he sits by the bride—he whispers her—he presses her hand. Sing now thy sweetest song, I beseech thee."

"But who are they on the opposite bank?" asked the Water Spirit.

"Thy lover's vassals only," answered the Dwarf.

"Be cheered, child!" said the Chief of Lörchausen. "See how the day smiles on us—thy bridegroom waits thee yonder—even now I see him towering above his comrades."

"Oh! my father, my heart sinks with fear!" murmured Unna; "and behold the frightful Lurlei Berg frowns upon us. Thou knowest how Rupert cautioned us to avoid it."

"And did we not, my child, because of that caution, embark yonder at the mouth of the Wisperbach? Even now our vessel glides towards the opposite shore, and nears not the mountain thy weak heart dreadest."

At that moment, a wild and most beautiful music broke tremulously along the waves; and they saw, sitting on the Lurlei Berg, a shape fairer than the shapes of the Children of Earth. "Hither," she sang, "hither, oh! gallant bark! Behold here is thy haven, and thy respite from the waters and the winds. Smooth is the surface of the tide around, and the rock hollows its bosom to receive thee. Hither, oh! nuptial band! The bridals are prepared. Here shall the betrothed gain the bridegroom, and the bridegroom welcome the bride!"

The boatmen paused, entranced with the air, the oars fell from their hands—the boat glided on towards the rock.

Rupert in dismay and terror heard the strain and recognized afar the silvery beauty of the Water Spirit. "Beware," he shouted—"beware—this way steer the vessel, not let it near to the Lurlei Berg."

Then the Dwarf laughed within himself, and he took up the sound ere it fell, and five times across the water, louder far than the bridegroom's voice, was repeated "Near to the Lurlei Berg."

At this time by the Gewirre opposite, the Dragon writhed his vast folds, and fierce and perilous whirled the waters round.

"See, my child," said the Chief of Lörchausen, "how the whirlpool foams and eddies on the opposite shore—wisely hath Sir Rupert dismissed superstition in the presence of real danger; and yon fair figure is doubtless stationed by his command to direct us how to steer from the whirlpool."

"Oh, no, no, my father!" cried Unna, clinging to his arm. "No, yon shape is but the false aspect of a fiend—I beseech you to put off from the Rock—see, we near—we near—its base!"

"Hark—hear ye not five voices telling us to near it!" answered the Chief; and he motioned to the rowers, who required no command to avoid the roar of the Gewirre.

"Death!" cried Rupert, stamping fiercely on the ground; "they heed me not!"—and he shouted again "Hither, for dear life's sake, hither!" And again, five times drowning his voice, came the echo from the Lurlei Berg, "For dear life's sake, hither!"

"Yes, hither!" sang once more the Water Spirit— "hither, O gallant bark!—as the brooklet to the river—as the bird to the sunny vine—flies the heart to the welcome of love!"

"Thou art avenged!" shouted the Dwarf, as he now stood visible and the boat strike suddenly among the shoals—and lo, in the smoothest waves it reeled once, and vanished beneath for ever! An eddy—a rush—and the Rhine flowed on without a sign of man upon its waves. "Lost, lost!" cried Rupert, clasping his hands, and five times from the Lurlei Berg echoed "Lost!"

And Rupert the Fearnought left his treasures and his castle, and the ruins still moulder to the nightly winds: and he sought the Sea-kings of the North; they fitted out a ship for the brave stranger, and he sailed on a distant cruize. And his name was a name of dread by the shores on which the fierce beak of his war-bark descended. And the bards rang it forth to their Runic harps over the blood-red wine. But at length they heard of his deeds no more—they traced not his whereabout—a sudden silence enwrapt him—his vessel had gone forth on a long voyage—it never returned, nor was heard of more. But still the undying Water Spirit mourns in her lonely caves—and still she fondly believes that the Wanderer will yet return. Often she sits, when the night is hushed, and the stars watch over the sleep of Earth, upon her desolate rock, and pours forth her melancholy strains. And yet the fishermen believe that she strives by her song to lure every raft and vessel that seems, to the deluded eyes of her passion, one which may contain her lover!

And still, too, when the Huntsman's horn sounds over the water—five times is the sound echoed from the Rock—the Dwarf himself may ever and anon be seen, in the new moon, walking on the heights of the Lurlei Berg, with a female form in an antique dress, devoutly believed to be the Lady of Lörchausen,—who, defrauded of a Knight, has reconciled herself to marriage with a Dwarf!

As to the moral of the tale, I am in doubt whether it is meant as a caution to heiresses or to singers; if the former, it is to be feared that the moral is not very efficacious, seeing that no less than three persons of that description have met with Ruperts within the last fortnight; but if to the latter, as in my own private opinion, it will be an encouragement to moralists ever after. Warned by the fate of their sister syren, those ladies take the most conscientious precautions, that, though they may sometimes be deserted, they should never at least be *impoverished*, by their lovers!

THE FALLEN STAR;
or the History of a False Religion

And the stars sat, each on his ruby throne, and watched with sleepless eyes upon the world. It was the night ushering in the new year, a night on which every star receives from the archangel that then visits the universal galaxy, its peculiar charge. The destinies of men and empires are then portioned forth for the coming year, and, unconsciously to ourselves, our fates become minioned to the stars. A hushed and solemn night is that in which the dark Gates of Time open to receive the ghost of the Dead Year, and the young and radiant Stranger rushed forth from the clouded chasms of Eternity. On that night, it is said, that there are given to the spirits that we see not, a privilege and a power; the dead are troubled in their forgotten graves, and men feast and laugh, while demon and angel are contending for their doom.

It was night in heaven; all was unutterably silent, the music of the spheres had paused, and not a sound came from the angels of the stars; and they who sat upon those shining thrones were three thousand and ten, each resembling each. Eternal youth clothed their radiant limbs with celestial beauty, and on their faces was written the dread of calm, that fearful stillness which feels not, sympathises not with the dooms over which it broods. War, tempest, pestilence, the rise of empires, and their fall, they ordain, they compass, unexultant and uncompassionate. The fell and thrilling crimes that stalk abroad when the world sleeps, the paricide with his stealthy step, and horrent brow, and lifted knife; the unwifed mother that glides out and looks behind, and behind, and shudders, and casts her babe upon the river, and hears the wail, and pities not—the splash, and does not tremble;—these the starred kings behold—to these they lead the unconscious step; but the guilt blanches not their lustre, neither doth remorse wither their unwrinkled youth. Each star wore a kingly diadem; round the loins of each was a graven belt, graven with many and mighty signs; and the foot of each was on a burning ball, and the right arm drooped over the knee as they bent down from their thrones; they moved not a limb or feature, save the finger of the right hand, which ever and anon moved slowly pointing, and regulated the fates of men as the hand of the dial speaks the career of time.

One only of the three thousand and ten wore not the same aspect as his crowned brethren, a star, smaller than the rest, and less luminous; the countenance of this star was not impressed with the awful calmness of the others; but there were sullenness and discontent upon his mighty brow.

And this star said to himself,—"Behold! I am created less glorious than my fellows, and the archangel apportions not to me the same lordly destinies. Not for me are the dooms of kings and bards, the rulers of empires, or, yet nobler, the swayers and harmonists of souls. Sluggish are the spirits and base the lots of the men I am ordained to lead through a dull life to a fameless grave. And wherefore?—is it mine own fault, or is it the fault which is not mine, that I was woven of beams less glorious than my brethren? Lo! when the archangel comes, I will bow not my crowned head to his decrees. I will speak, as the ancestral Lucifer before me: *he* rebelled because of his glory, I because of my obscurity; *he* from the ambition of pride, and I from its discontent."

And while the star was thus communing with himself, the upward heavens were parted as by a long river of light, and adown that stream swiftly, and without sound, sped the archangel visitor of the star; his vast limbs floated in the liquid lustre, and his outspread wings, each plume the glory of a sun, bore him noiselessly along; but thick clouds veiled his lustre from the eyes of mortals, and while above all was bathed in the serenity of his splendour, tempest and storm broke below over the children of the earth: "He bowed the heavens and came down, darkness was under his feet."

And the stillness on the faces of the stars became yet more still, and the awfulness was humbled into awe. Right above their thrones paused the course of the archangel; and his wings stretched from east to west, overshadowing with the shadow of light the immensity of space. Then forth, in the shining stillness, rolled the dread music of his voice: and, fulfilling the heraldry of God, to each star he appointed the duty and the charge, and each star bowed his head yet lower as he heard the fiat, while his throne rocked and trembled at the Majesty of the Word. But, at last, when each of the brighter stars had, in succession, received the mandate, and the vice-royalty over the nations of the earth, the purple and diadems of kings;—the archangel addressed the less star as he sat apart from his fellows:—

"Behold," said the archangel, "the rude tribes of the north, the fishermen of the river that flows beneath, and the hunters of the forests, that darken the mountain tops with verdure! these be thy charge, and their destinies thy care. Nor deem thou, O Star of the sullen beams, that thy duties are less glorious than the duties of thy brethren; for the peasant is not less to thy master and mine than the monarch; nor doth the doom of empires rest more upon the sovereign than on the herd. The passions and the heart are the dominion of the stars,—a mighty realm; nor less mighty beneath the hide that garbs the shepherd, than under the jewelled robes of the eastern kings."

Then the star lifted his pale front from his breast, and answered the archangel:—

"Lo!" he said, "ages had passed, and each year thou hast appointed me to the same ignoble charge. Release me, I pray thee, from the duties that I scorn; or, if thou wilt that the lowlier race of men be my charge, give unto me the charge not of many, but of one, and suffer me to breathe into him the desire that spurns the valleys of life, and ascends its steeps. If the humble are given to me, let there be amongst them one whom I may lead on the mission that shall abase the proud; for, behold, O Appointer of the Stars, as I have sat for uncounted years upon my solitary throne, brooding over the things beneath, my spirit hath gathered wisdom from the changes that shift below. Looking upon the tribes of earth, I have seen how the multitude are swayed, and tracked the steps that lead weakness into power; and fain would I be the ruler of one who, if abased, shall aspire to rule."

As a sudden cloud over the face of noon was the change on the brow of the archangel.

"Proud and melancholy star," said the herald, "thy wish would war with the courses of the invisible DESTINY, that, thronged far above, sways and harmonises all; the source from which the lesser rivers of fate are eternally gushing through the heart of the universe of things. Thinkest thou that thy wisdom, of itself, can lead the peasant to become a king?"

And the crowned star gazed undauntedly on the face of the archangel, and answered,

"Yea!—grant me but one trial!"

Ere the archangel could reply, the farthest centre of the heaven was rent as by a thunderbolt; and the divine herald covered his face with his hands, and a voice low and sweet, and mild with the consciousness of unquestionable power, spoke forth to the repining star.

"The time has arrived when thou mayest have thy wish. Below thee, upon yon solitary plain, sits a mortal, gloomy as thyself, who, born under thy influence, may be moulded to thy will."

The voice ceased as the voice of a dream. Silence was over the seas of space, and the archangel, once more borne aloft, slowly soared away into the farther heaven, to promulgate the divine bidding to the stars of far-distant worlds. But the soul of the discontented star exulted within itself; and it said, "I will call forth a king from the valley of the herdsman, that shall trample on the kings subject to my fellows, and render the charge of the condemned star more glorious than the minions of its favoured brethren; thus shall I revenge neglect—thus shall I prove my claim hereafter to the heritage of the great of earth!"

At that time, though the world had rolled on for ages, and the pilgrimage of man had passed through various states of existence, which our dim traditionary knowledge has not preserved, yet the condition of our race in the northern hemisphere was then what *we,* in our imperfect love, have conceived to be among the earliest.

By a rude and vast pile of stones, the masonry of arts forgotten, a lonely man sat at midnight, gazing upon the heavens, a storm had just passed from the earth—the clouds had rolled away, and the high stars looked down upon the rapid waters of the Rhine; and no sound save the roar of the waves, and the dripping of the rain from the mighty trees, was heard around the ruined pile: the white sheep lay scattered on the plain, and slumber with them. He sat watching over the herd, lest the foes of a neighbouring tribe seized them unawares, and thus he communed with himself: "The king sits upon his throne, and is honoured by a warrior race, and the warrior exults in the trophies he has won; the step of the huntsman is bold upon the mountain-top, and his name is sung at night round the pine-fires, by the lips of the bard; and the bard himself hath honour in the hall. But I, who belong not to the race of kings, and whose limbs can bound not to the rapture of war, nor scale the eyries of the eagle and the haunts of the swift stag; whose hand cannot string the harp, and whose voice is harsh in the song; I have neither honour nor command, and men bow not the head as I pass along; yet do I feel within me the consciousness of a great power that should rule my species—not obey. My eye pierces the secret hearts of men—I see their thoughts ere their lips proclaim them; and I scorn, while I see, the weakness and the vices which I never shared—I laugh at the madness of the warrior—I mock within my soul at the tyranny of kings. Surely there is something in man's nature more fitted to command—more worthy of renown, than the sinews of the arm, or the swiftness of the feet, or the accident of birth!"

As Morven, the son of Osslah, thus mused within himself, still looking at the heavens, the solitary man beheld a star suddenly shooting from its place, and speeding through the silent air, till it suddenly paused right over the midnight river, and facing the inmate of the pile of stones.

As he gazed upon the star, strange thoughts grew slowly over him. He drank, as it were, from its solemn aspect, the spirit of a great design. A dark cloud rapidly passing over the earth, snatched the star from his sight; but left to his awakened mind the thoughts and the dim scheme that had come to him as he gazed.

When the sun arose, one of his brethren relieved him of his charge over the herd, and he went away, but not to his father's home. Musingly he plunged into the dark and leafless recesses of the winter forest; and shaped out of his wild thoughts, more palpably and clearly, the outline of his daring hope. While thus absorbed, he heard a great noise in the forest, and, fearful lest the hostile tribe of the Alrich might pierce that way, he ascended one of the loftiest pine-trees, to whose perpetual verdure the winter had not denied the shelter he sought, and concealed by its branches, he looked anxiously forth in the direction when the noise had proceeded. And IT came—it came with a tramp and a crash, and a crushing tread upon the crunched boughs and matted leaves that strewed the soil—it came—it came, the monster that the world now holds no more—the mighty Mammoth[1] of the North! Slowly it moved its huge strength along, and its burning eyes glittered through the gloomy shade; its jaws, falling apart, showed the grinders with which it snapped asunder the young oaks of the forest; and the vast tusks, which, curved downward to the midst of its massive limbs, glistened white and ghastly, curdling the blood of one destined hereafter to be the dreadest ruler of the men of that distant age.

❧   The livid eyes of the monster fastened on the form of the herdsman, even amidst the thick darkness of the pine. It paused—it glared upon him—its jaws opened, and a low deep sound as of

51

gathering thunder, seemed to the son of Osslah as the knell of a dreadful grave. But after glaring on him for some moments, it again, and calmly, pursued its terrible way, crashing the boughs as it marched along, till the last sound of its heavy tread died away upon his ear.

Ere yet, however, Morven summoned the courage to descend the tree, he saw the shining of arms through the bare branches of the wood, and presently a small band of the hostile Alrich came into sight. He was perfectly hidden from them; and, listening as they passed him, he heard one say to another, —

"The night covers all things; why attack them by day?"

And he who seemed the chief of the band, answered,

"Right. To-night, when they sleep in their city, we will upon them. Lo! they will be drenched in wine, and fall like sheep into our hands."

"But where, O chief," said a third of the band, "shall our men hide during the day? for there are many hunters among the youth of the Oestrich tribe and they might see us in the forest unawares, and arm their race against our coming."

"I have prepared for that," answered the chief. "Is not the dark cavern of Oderlin at hand? Will it not shelter us from the eyes of the victims?"

Then the men laughed, and, shouting, they went their way adown the forest.

When they were gone, Morven cautiously descended, and, striking into a broad path, hastened to a vale that lay between the forest and the river in which was the city where the chief of his country dwelt. As he passed by the warlike men, giants in that day[2], who thronged the streets (if streets they might be called), their half garments parting from their huge limbs, the quiver at their backs, and the hunting spear in their hands, they laughed and shouted out, and, pointing to him, cried, "Morven, the woman! Morven, the cripple! what dost thou among men?"

For the son of Osslah was small in stature and of slender strength, and his step had halted from his birth; but he passed through the warriors unheedingly. At the outskirts of the city he came upon a tall pile in which some old men dwelt by themselves, and counselled the king when times of danger, or when the failure of the season, the famine or the drought, perplexed the ruler, and clouded the savage fronts of his warrior tribe.

They gave the counsels of experience, and when experience

52

failed, they drew in their believing ignorance, assurances, and omens from the winds of heaven, the changes of the moon, and the flight of the wandering birds. Filled (by the voices of the elements, and the variety of mysteries which ever shift along the face of things, unsolved by the wonder which pauses not, the fear which believes, and that eternal reasoning of all experience, which assigns causes to effect) with the notion of superior powers, they assisted their ignorance by the conjectures of their superstition. But as yet they knew no craft and practised no *voluntary* delusion; they trembled too much at the mysteries which had created their faith to seek to belie them. They counselled as they believed, and the bold dream of governing their warriors and their kings by the wisdom of deceit had never dared to cross men thus worn and grey with age.

The son of Osslah entered the vast pile with a fearless step, and approached the place at the upper end of the hall where the old men sat in conclave.

"How, base-born and craven limbed!" cried the eldest, who had been a noted warrior in his day; "darest thou enter unsummoned amidst the secret councils of the wise men? Knowest thou not, scatterling! that the penalty is death?"

"Slay me, if thou wilt," answered Morven, "but hear! As I sat last night in the ruined palace of our ancient kings, tending, as my father bade me, the sheep that grazed around, lest the fierce tribe of Alrich should descend unseen from the mountains upon the herd, a storm came darkly on; and when the storm had ceased, and I looked above on the sky, I saw a star descend from its height towards me, and a voice from the star said, 'Son of Osslah, leave thy herd and seek the council of the wise men, and say unto them, that they take thee as one of them and theirs.' But I had courage to answer the voice, and I said, 'Mock not the poor son of the herdsman. Behold they will kill me if I utter so rash a word, for I am poor and valueless in the eyes of the tribe of Oestrich, and the great in deeds and the grey of hair alone sit in the council of the wise men.'

"Then the voice said, 'Do my bidding, and I will give thee a token that thou comest from the Powers that sway the seasons and sail upon the eagles of the winds. Say unto the wise men that this very night, if they refuse to receive thee of their band, evil shall fall upon them, and the morrow shall dawn in blood.'

"Then the voice ceased, and the cloud passed over the star;

and I communed with myself, and came, O dread fathers, mournfully unto you. For I feared that ye would smite me because of my bold tongue, and that ye would sentence me to the death, in that I asked what may scarce be given even to the sons of kings."

Then the grim elders looked one at the other, and marvelled much, nor know they what answer they should make to the herdsman's son.

At length one of the wise men said, "Surely there must be truth in the son of Osslah, for he would not dare to falsify the great lights of Heaven. If he had given unto men the words of the star, verily we might doubt the truth. But who would brave the vengeance of the gods of night?"

Then the elders shook their heads approvingly; but one answered and said —

"Shall we take the herdsman's son as our equal? No!" The name of the man who thus answered was Darvan, and his words were pleasing to the elders.

But Morven spoke out: "Of a truth, O councillors of kings! I look not to be an equal with yourselves. Enough if I tend the gates of your palace, and serve you as the son of Osslah may serve;" and he bowed his head humbly as he spoke.

Then said the chief of the elders, for he was wiser than the others, "But how wilt thou deliver us from the evil that is to come? Doubtless the star has informed thee of the service thou canst render to us if we take thee into our palace, as well as the ill that will fall on us if we refuse."

Morven answered meekly, "Surely, if thou acceptest thy servant, the star will teach him that which may requite thee; but as yet he knows only what he has uttered."

Then the sages bade him withdraw, and they communed with themselves, and they differed much; but though fierce men, and bold at the war-cry of a human foe, they shuddered at the prophecy of a star. So they resolved to take the son of Osslah, and suffer him to keep the gate of the council-hall.

He heard their decree and bowed his head, and went to the gate, and sat down by it in silence.

And the sun went down in the west, and the first star of the twilight began to glimmer, when Morven started from his seat, and a trembling appeared to seize his limbs. His lips foamed; an agony and a fear possessed him; he writhed as a man whom the spear of a foeman has pierced with a mortal wound, and suddenly fell upon his face on the stony earth.

The elders approached him; wondering, they lifted him up. He slowly recovered as from a swoon; his eyes rolled wildly.

"Heard ye not the voice of the star?" he said.

And the chief of the elders answered, "Nay, we heard no sound."

Then Morven sighed heavily.

"To me only the word was given. Summon instantly, O councillors of the king! summon the armed men, and all the youth of the tribe, and let them take the sword and the spear, and follow thy servant. For lo! the star hath announced to him that the foe shall fall into our hands as the wild beast of the forests."

The son of Osslah spoke with the voice of command, and the elders were amazed. "Why pause ye?" he cried. "Do the gods of the night lie? On my head rest the peril if I deceive ye."

Then the elders communed together; and they went forth and summoned the men of arms, and all the young of the tribe; and each man took the sword and the spear, and Morven also. And the son of Osslah walked first, still looking up at the star, and he motioned them to be silent, and move with a stealthy step.

So they went through the thickest of the forest, till they came to the mouth of a great cave, overgrown with aged and matted trees, and it was called the Cave of Oderlin; and he bade the leaders place the armed men on either side the cave, to the right and to the left, among the bushes.

So they watched silently till the night deepened, when they heard a noise in the cave and the sound of feet, and forth came an armed man; and the spear of Morven pierced him, and he fell dead at the mouth of the cave. Another and another, and both fell! Then loud and long was heard the war-cry of Alrich, and forth poured as a stream over a narrow bed, the river of armed men. And the sons of Oestrich fell upon them, and the foe were sorely perplexed and terrified by the suddenness of the battle and the darkness of the night; and there was a great slaughter.

And when the morning came, the children of Oestrich counted the slain, and found the leader of Alrich and the chief men of the tribe among them, and great was the joy thereof. So they went back in triumph to the city, and they carried the brave son of Osslah on their shoulders, and shouted forth, "Glory to the servant of the star."

And Morven dwelt in the council of the wise men.

Now the king of the tribe had one daughter, and she was stately amongst the women of the tribe, and fair to look upon. And Morven gazed upon her with the eyes of love, but he did not dare to speak.

Now the son of Osslah laughed secretly at the foolishness of men, he loved them not, for they had mocked him; he honoured them not, for he had blinded the wisest of their elders. He shunned their feasts and merriment, and lived apart and solitary. The austerity of his life increased the mysterious homage which his commune with the stars had won him, and the boldest of the warriors bowed his head to the favourite of the gods.

One day he was wandering by the side of the river, and he saw a large bird of prey rise from the waters, and give chase to a hawk that had not gained the full strength of its wings. From his youth the solitary Morven had loved to watch, in the great forests and by the banks of the mighty stream, the habits of the things which nature has submitted to man; and looking now on the birds, he said to himself, "Thus is it ever; by cunning or by strength each thing wishes to master its kind." While thus moralising, the larger bird had stricken down the hawk, and it fell terrified and panting at his feet. Morven took the hawk in his hands, and the vulture shrieked above him, wheeling nearer and nearer to its protected prey; but Morven scared away the vulture, and placing the hawk in his bosom he carried it home, and tended it carefully, and fed it from his hand until it had regained its strength; and the hawk knew him, and followed him as a dog. And Morven said, smiling to himself, "Behold, the credulous fools around me put faith in the flight and motion of birds. I will teach this poor hawk to minister to my ends." So he tamed the bird, and tutored it according to its nature; but he concealed it carefully from others, and cherished it in secret.

The king of the country was old and like to die, and the eyes of the tribe were turned to his two sons, nor knew they which was the worthier to reign. And Morven passing through the forest one evening, saw the younger of the two, who was a great hunter, sitting mournfully under an oak, and looking with musing eyes upon the ground.

"Wherefore musest thou, O swift-footed Siror?" said the son of Osslah; "and wherefore art thou sad?"

"Thou canst not assist me," answered the prince, sternly; "take thy way."

"Nay," answered Morven, "thou knowest not what thou sayest; am I not the favourite of the stars?"

"Away, I am no greybeard whom the approach of death makes doting: talk not to me of the stars; I know only the things that my eye sees and my ear drinks in."

"Hush," said Morven, solemnly, and covering his face; "hush! lest the heavens avenge thy rashness. But behold, the stars have given unto me to piece the secret hearts of others; and I can tell thee the thoughts of thine."

"Speak out, base-born!"

"Thou are the younger of two, and thy name is less known in war than the name of thy brother: yet wouldst thou desire to be set over his head, and to sit on the high seat of thy father?"

The young man turned pale. "Thou hast truth in thy lips," said he, with a faltering voice.

"Not from me, but from the stars, descends the truth."

"Can the stars grant my wish?"

"They can: let us meet to-morrow." Thus saying, Morven passed into the forest.

The next day, at noon, they met again.

"I have consulted the gods of night, and they have given me the power that I prayed for, but on one condition."

"Name it."

"That thou sacrifice thy sister on their altars; thou must build a heap of stones, and take thy sister into the wood, and lay her on the pile, and plunge thy sword into her heart; so only shalt thou reign."

The prince shuddered, and started to his feet, and shook his spear at the pale front of Morven.

"Tremble," said the son of Osslah, with a loud voice. "Hark to the gods who threaten thee with death, that thou hast dared to lift thine arm against their servant!"

As he spoke, the thunder rolled above; for one of the frequent storms of the early summer was about to break. The spear dropped from the prince's hand; he sat down, and cast his eyes on the ground.

"Wilt thou do the bidding of the star, and reign?" said Morven.

"I will!" cried Siror, with a desperate voice.

"This evening, then, when the sun sets, thou wilt lead her

hither, alone; I may not attend thee. Now, let us pile the stones."

Silently the huntsman bent his vast strength to the fragments of rock that Morven pointed to him, and they built the altar, and went their way.

And beautiful is the dying of the great sun, when the last song of the birds fades into the lap of silence; when the islands of the cloud are bathed in light, and the first star springs up over the grave of day!

"Whither leadest thou my steps, my brother?" said Orna; "and why doth thy lip quiver? and why dost thou turn away thy face?"

"Is not the forest beautiful, does it not tempt us forth, my sister?"

"And wherefore are those heaps of stone piled together?"

"Let others answer; I piled them not."

"Thou tremblest, brother: we will return."

"Not so; by those stones is a bird that my shaft pierced to-day; a bird of beautiful plumage that I slew for thee."

"We are by the pile: where hast thou laid the bird?"

"Here!" cried Siror; and seized the maiden in his arms, and, casting her on the rude altar, he drew forth his sword to smite her to the heart.

Right over the stones rose a giant oak, the growth of immemorial ages; and from the oak, or from the heavens, broke forth a loud and solemn voice, "Strike not, son of kings! the stars forbear their own: the maiden thou shalt not slay; yet shalt thou reign over the race of Oestrich; and thou shalt give Orna as a bride to the favourite of the stars. Arise, and go thy way!"

The voice ceased: the terror of Orna had overpowered for a time the springs of life; and Siror bore her home through the wood in his strong arms.

"Alas!" said Morven, when, at the next day, he again met the aspiring prince; "alas! the stars have ordained me a lot which my heart desires not: for I, lonely of life, and crippled of shape, am insensible to the fires of love; and ever, as thou and thy tribe know, I have shunned the eyes of women, for the maidens laughed at my halting step and my sullen features; and so in my youth I learned betimes to banish all thoughts of love. But since they told me (as they declared to *thee*), that only through that marriage, thou, O beloved prince! canst obtain thy father's plumed crown, I yield me to their will."

"But," said the prince, "not until I am king can I give thee my sister in marriage; for thou knowest that my sire would smite me to the dust, if I asked him to give the flower of our race to the son of the herdsman Osslah."

"Thou speakest the words of truth. Go home and fear not: but, when thou art king, the sacrifice must be made, and Orna mine. Alas! how can I dare to lift my eyes to her! But so ordain the dread kings of the night!—who shall gainsay their word?"

"The day that sees me king, sees Orna thine," answered the prince.

Morven walked forth, as was his wont, alone; and he said to himself, "The king is old, yet may he live long between me and mine hope!" and he began to cast in his mind how he might shorten the time. Thus absorbed, he wandered on so unheedingly, that night advanced, and he had lost his path among the thick woods, and knew not how to regain his home: so he lay down quietly beneath a tree, and rested till day dawned; then hunger came upon him, and he searched among the bushes for such simple roots as those with which, for he was ever careless of food, he was used to appease the cravings of nature.

He found, among other more familiar herbs and roots, a red berry of a sweetish taste, which he had never observed before. He ate of it sparingly, and had not proceeded far in the wood before he found his eyes swim and a deadly sickness came over him. For several hours he lay convulsed on the ground expecting death; but the gaunt spareness of his frame, and his unvarying abstinence, prevailed over the poison, and he recovered slowly, and after great anguish: but he went with feeble steps back to the spot where the berries grew, and, plucking several, hid them in his bosom, and by nightfall regained the city.

The next day he went forth among his father's herds, and seizing a lamb, forced some of the berries into his stomach, and the lamb, escaping, ran away, and fell down dead. Then Morven took some more of the berries and boiled them down, and mixed the juice with wine, and he gave the wine in secret to one of his father's servants, and the servant died.

Then Morven sought the king, and coming into his presence alone, he said unto him, "How fares my lord?"

The king sat on a couch, made of the skins of wolves, and his eye was glassy and dim; but vast were his aged limbs, and huge was his stature, and he had been taller by a head than the children of men, and none living could bend the bow he had bent in youth. Grey, gaunt, and worn, as some mighty bones that are dug at time from the bosom of the earth, a relic of the strength of old.

And the king said, faintly and with a ghastly laugh,—

"The men of my years fare ill. What avails my strength? Better had I been born a cripple like thee, so should I have had nothing to lament in growing old."

The red flush passed over Morven's brow; but he bent humbly,—

"O king, what if I could give thee back thy youth? what if I could restore to thee the vigour which distinguished thee above the sons of men, when the warriors of Alrich fell like grass before thy sword?"

Then the king uplifted his dull eyes, and he said,—

"What meanest thou, son of Osslah? Surely I hear much of thy great wisdom, and how thou speakest nightly with the star. Can the gods of the night give unto thee the secret to make the old young?"

"Tempt them not by doubt," said Morven, reverently. "All things are possible to the rulers of the dark hour; and, lo! the star that loves thy servant spake to him at the dead of night, and said, 'Arise, and go unto the king; and tell him that the stars honour the tribe of Oestrich, and remember how the king bent his bow against the sons of Alrich; wherefore, look thou under the stone that lies to the right of thy dwelling—even beside the pine-tree, and thou shalt see a vessel of clay, and in the vessel thou wilt find a sweet liquid, that shall make the king thy master forget his age for ever.' Therefore, my lord, when the morning rose I went forth, and looked under the stone, and behold the vessel of clay; and I have brought it hither to my lord, the king."

"Quick—slave—quick! that I may drink and regain my youth!"

"Nay, listen, O king! father said the star to me:

" 'It is only at night, when the stars have power, that this their gift will avail; wherefore, the king must wait till the hush of the midnight, when the moon is high, and then may he mingle the liquid with his wine. And he must reveal to none that he hath received the gift from the hand of the servant of the stars. For THEY do their work in secret, and when men sleep therefore they love not the babble of mouths, and he who reveals their benefits shall surely die.' "

"Fear not," said the king, grasping the vessel; "none shall know: and, behold, I will rise on the morrow; and my two sons—wrangling for my crown,—verily I shall be younger than they!"

Then the king laughed loud; and he scarcely thanked the servant of the stars, neither did he promise him reward: for the kings in those days had little thought,—save for themselves.

And Morven said to him, "Shalt I not attend my lord? for without me, perchance, the drug might fail of its effect."

"Ay," said the king, "rest here."

"Nay," replied Morven; "thy servants will marvel and talk much, if they see the son of Osslah sojourning in thy palace. So would the displeasure of the gods of night perchance be incurred. Suffer that the lesser door of the palace be unbarred, so that at the night hour, when the moon is midway in the heavens, I may steal unseen into thy chamber, and mix the liquid with they wine."

"So be it," said the king. "Thou art wise, though thy limbs are crooked and curt; and the stars might have chosen a taller man." Then the king laughed again; and Morven laughed too, but there was danger in the mirth of the son of Osslah.

The night had begun to wane, and the inhabitants of Oestrich were buried in deep sleep, when, hark! a sharp voice was heard crying out in the streets, "Woe, woe! Awake, ye sons of Ostrich—woe!" Then forth, wild—haggard—alarmed —spear in hand, rushed the giant sons of the rugged tribe, and they saw a man on a height in the middle of the city, shrieking "Woe!" and it was Morven, the son of Osslah! And he said unto them as they gathered round him, "Men and warriors, tremble as ye hear. The star of the west hath spoken to me, and thus said the star:—'Evil shall fall upon the kingly house of Oestrich,—yea, ere the morning dawn; wherefore, go thou mourning into the streets, and wake the inhabitants to woe!' So I rose and did the bidding of the star;" And while Morven was yet speaking, a servant of the king's house ran up to the crowd, crying loudly—"The king is dead!" So they went into the palace and found the king stark upon his couch, and his huge limbs all cramped and crippled by the pangs of death, and his hands clenched as if in menace of a foe—the Foe of all living flesh! Then fear came on the gazers, and they looked on Morven with a deeper awe than the boldest warrior would have called forth; and they bore him back to the council-hall of the wise men, wailing and clashing their arms in woe, and shouting, ever and anon, "Honour to

Morven the prophet!" And that was the first time the word PROPHET was ever used in those countries.

At noon, on the third day from the king's death, Siror sought Morven, and he said, "Lo, my father is no more, and the people meet this evening at sunset to elect his successor, and the warriors and the young men will surely choose my brother, for he is more known in war. Fail me not, therefore."

"Peace, boy!" said Morven, sternly; "nor dare to question the truth of the gods of night."

For Morven now began to presume on his power among the people, and to speak as rulers speak, even to the sons of kings. And the voice silenced the fiery Siror, nor dared he to reply.

"Behold," said Morven, taking up a chaplet of coloured plumes, "wear this on they head, and put on a brave face, for the people like a hopeful spirit, and go down with thy brother to the place where the new king is to be chosen, and leave the rest to the stars. But, above all things, forget not that chaplet; it has been blessed by the gods of night."

The prince took the chaplet and returned home.

It was evening, and the warriors and chiefs of the tribe were assembled in the place where the new king was to be elected. And the voices of the many favoured Prince Voltoch, the brother of Siror, for he had slain twelve foemen with his spear; and verily, in those days, that was a great virtue in a king.

Suddenly there was a shout in the streets, and the people cried out, "Way for Morven the prophet, the prophet!" For the people held the son of Osslah in even greater respect that did the chiefs. Now, since he had become of note, Morven had assumed a majesty of air which the son of the herdsman knew not in his earlier days; and albeit his stature was short, and his limbs halted, yet his coutenance was grave and high. He only of the tribe wore a garment that swept the ground, and his head was bare, and his long black hair descended to his girdle, and rarely was change or human passion seen in his calm aspect. He feared not, nor drank wine, nor was his presence frequent in the streets. He laughed not, neither did he smile, save when alone in the forest,—and then he laughed at the follies of his tribe.

So he walked slowly through the crowd, neither turning to the left nor to the right, as the crowd gave way; and he supported his steps with a staff of the knotted pine.

And when he came to the place where the chiefs were met, and the two princes stood in the centre, he bade the people around him proclaim silence; then mounting on a huge fragment of rock, he thus spake to the multitude:—

"Princes, Warriors, and Bards! ye, O council of the wise men! and ye O hunters of the forests, and snarers of the fishes of the streams! hearken to Morven, the son of Osslah. Ye know that I am lowly of race, and weak of limb; but did I not give into your hands the tribe of Alrich, and did ye not slay them in the dead of night with a great slaughter? Surely, ye must know this of himself did not the herdsman's son; surely he was but the agent of the bright gods that love the children of Oestrich? three nights since when slumber was on the earth, was not my voice heard in the streets! Did I not proclaim woe to the kingly house of Oestrich! and verily the dark arm had fallen on the bosom of the mighty, that is no more. Could I have dreamed this thing merely in a dream, or was I not as the voice of the bright gods that watch over the tribes of Oestrich? Wherefore, O men and chiefs! scorn not the son of Osslah, but listen to his words; for are they not the wisdom of the stars? Behold, last night, I sat alone in the valley, and the trees were hushed around and not a breath stirred; and I looked upon the star that counsels the son of Osslah; and I said, 'Dread conqueror of the cloud! thou that bathest thy beauty in the streams and piercest the pine-boughs with thy presence; behold thy servant grieved because the mighty one hath passed away, and many foes surround the houses of my brethren; and it is well that they should have a king valiant and prosperous in war, the cherished of the stars. Wherefore, O star! as thou gavest into our hands the warriors of Alrich, and didst warn us of the fall of the oak of our tribe, wherefore I pray thee give unto the people a token that they may choose that king whom the gods of the night prefer!' Then a low voice, sweeter than the music of the bard, stole along the silence. "Thy love for thy race is grateful to the star of night: go, then, son of Osslah, and seek the meeting of the chiefs and the people to choose a king, and tell them not to scorn thee because thou art slow to the chase, and little known in war; for the stars give thee wisdom as a recompense for all. Say unto the people that as the wise men of the council shape their lessons by the flight of birds, so by the flight of birds shall a token be given unto them, and they shall choose their kings. For, saith the star of night, the birds are the children of the winds, they pass to and fro along the ocean of the air, and visit the clouds that are the war-ships of the gods. And their music is but broken melodies which they glean from the harps above. Are they not the messengers of the storm? Ere the stream chafes against the bank, and the rain descends, know ye not, by the wail of birds and their low circles over the earth, that the tempest is at hand? Wherefore, wisely do ye deem that the children of the air are the fit interpreters between the sons of men and the lords of the world above. Say then to the people and the chiefs, that they shall take, from among the doves that build their nests in the roof of the palace, a white dove, and they shall let it loose in the air, and verily the gods of the night shall deem the dove as a prayer coming from the people, and they shall send a messenger to grant the prayer and give to the tribes of Oestrich a king worthy of themselves.'

"With that the star spoke no more."

Then the friends of Voltoch murmured among themselves, and they said, "Shall this man dictate to us who shall be king?" But the people and the warriors shouted, "Listen to the star; do we not give or deny battle according as the bird flies,—shall we not by the same token choose him by whom the battle should be led?" And the thing seemed natural to them, for it was after the custom of the tribe. Then they took one of the doves that built in the roof of the palace, and they brought it to the spot where Morven stood, and he, looking up to the stars and muttering to himself, released the bird.

There was a copse of trees at a little distance from the spot, and as the dove ascended, a hawk suddenly rose from the copse and pursued the dove; and the dove was terrified, and soared circling high above the crowd, when lo, the hawk, poising itself one moment on its wings, swooped with a sudden swoop, and, abandoning its pray, alighted on the plumed head of Siror.

"Behold," cried Morven in a loud voice, "behold your king!"

"Hail, all hail the king!" shouted the people. "All hail the chosen of the stars!"

Then Morven lifted his right hand, and the hawk left the prince and alighted on Morven's shoulder. "Bird of the gods!" said he, reverently, "hast thou not a secret message for my ear?" Then the hawk put its beak to Morven's ear, and Morven bowed his head submissively; and the hawk rested with Morven from that moment and would not be scared away. And Morven said, "The stars have sent me this bird, that, in the day-time when I see them not, we may never be without a councillor in distress."

So Siror was made king, and Morven the son of Osslah was constrained by the king's will to take Orna for his wife; and the people and the chiefs honoured Morven the prophet above all the elders of the tribe.

One day Morven said unto himself, musing, "Am I not already equal with the king! nay, is not the king my servant? did I not place him over the heads of his brother? am I not, therefore, more fit to reign than he is? shall I not push him from his seat? It is a troublesome and stormy office to reign over the wild men of Oestrich, to feast in the crowded hall, and to lead the warriors to the fray. Surely if I feasted not, neither went out to war, they might say, this is no king, but the cripple Morven; and some of the race of Siror might slay me secretly. But can I not be greater far than kings, and continue to choose and govern them, living as now at my own ease? Verily the stars shall give me a new palace, and many subjects."

Among the wise men was Darvan; and Morven feared him, for his eye often sought the movements of the son of Osslah.

And Morven said, "It were better to *trust* this man than to *blind,* for surely I want a helpmate and a friend." So he said to the wise man as he sat alone watching the setting sun.

"It seemeth to me, O Darvan! that we ought to build a great pile in honour of the stars, and the pile should be more glorious than all the palaces of the chiefs and the palace of the king; for are not the stars our masters? And thou and I should be the chief dwellers in this new palace, and we would serve the gods of night and fatten their altars with the choicest of the herd, and the freshest of the fruits of the earth."

And Darvan said, "Thou speakest as becomes the servant of the stars. But will the people help to build the pile, for they are a warlike race and they love not toil?"

And Morven answered, "Doubtless the stars will ordain the work to be done. Fear not."

"In truth thou art a wondrous man, thy words ever come to pass," answered Darvan; "and I wish thou wouldest teach me, friend, the language of the stars."

"Assuredly if thou servest me, thou shalt know," answered the proud Morven; and Darvan was secretly wroth that the son of the herdsman should command the service of an elder and a chief.

And when Morven returned to his wife he found her weeping much. Now she loved the son of Osslah with an exceeding love, for he was not savage and fierce as the men she had known, and she was proud of his fame among the tribe; and he took her in his arms and kissed her, and asked her why she wept. Then she told him that her brother the king had visited her and had spoken bitter words of Morven: "He taketh from me the affection of my people," said Siror, "and blindeth them with lies. And since he hath made me king, what if he take my kingdom from me? Verily a new tale of the stars might undo the old." And the king had ordered her to keep watch on Morven's secrecy, and to see whether truth was in him when he boasted of his commune with the Powers of night.

But Orna loved Morven better than Siror, therefore she told her husband all.

And Morven resented the king's ingratitude, and was troubled much, for a king is a powerful foe; but he comforted Orna, and bade her dissemble, and complain also of him to her brother, so that he might confide to her unsuspectingly whatsoever he might design against Morven.

There was a cave by Morven's house in which he kept the sacred hawk, and wherein he secretly trained and nurtured other birds against future need, and the door of the cave was always barred. And one day he was thus engaged when he beheld a chink in the wall, that he had never noted before, and the sun came playfully in; and while he looked he perceived the sunbeam was darkened, and presently he saw a human face peering in through the chink. And Morven trembled, for he knew he had been watched. He ran hastily from the cave, but the spy had disappeared amongst the trees, and Morven went straight to the chamber of Darvan and sat himself down. And Darvan did not return home till late, and he started and turned pale when he saw Morven. But Morven greeted him as a brother, and bade him to a feast, which, for the first time, he purposed giving at the full of the moon, in honour of the stars. And going out of Darvan's chamber he returned to his wife, and bade her rend her hair, and go at the dawn of day to the king her brother, and complain bitterly of Morven's treatment, and pluck the black plans from the breast of the king. "For surely," said he, "Darvan hath lied to thy brother, and some evil waits me that I would fain know."

So the next morning Orna sought the king, and she said, "The herdsman's son hath reviled me, and spoken harsh words to me; shall I not be avenged?"

Then the king stamped his feet and shook his mighty sword. "Surely thou shalt be avenged, for I have learned from one of the elders that which convinceth me that the man hath lied to the people, and the base-born shall surely die. Yea, the first time that he goeth alone into the forest my brother and I will fall upon him, and smite him to the death." And with this comfort Siror dismissed Orna.

And Orna flung herself at the feet of her husband. "Fly now, O my beloved!—fly into the forests afar from my brethren, or surely the sword of Siror will end thy days."

Then the son of Osslah folded his arms, and seemed buried in black thoughts; nor did he heed the voice of Orna, until again and again she had implored him to fly.

"Fly!" he said at length. "Nay, I was doubting what punishment the stars should pour down upon our foe. Let warriors fly. Morven the prophet conquers by arms mightier than the sword."

Nevertheless Morven was perplexed in his mind, and knew not how to save himself from the vengeance of the king. Now, while he was musing hopelessly, he heard a roar of waters; and behold the river, for it was now the end of autumn, had burst its bounds, and was rushing along the valley to the houses of the city. And now the men of the tribe, and the women, and the children, came running, and with shrieks to Morven's house, crying, "Behold the river has burst upon us!—Save us, O ruler of the stars!"

Then the sudden thought broke upon Morven, and he resolved to risk his fate upon one desperate scheme.

And he came out from the house calm and sad, and he said, "Ye know not what ye ask; I cannot save ye from this peril: ye have brought it on yourselves."

And they cried, "How? O son of Osslah!—we are ignorant of our crime."

And he answered, "Go down to the king's palace and wait before it, and surely I will follow ye, and ye shall learn wherefore ye have incurred this punishment from the gods." Then the crowd rolled murmuring back, as a receding sea; and when it was gone from the place, Morven went along to the house of Darvan, which was next his own: and Darvan was greatly terrified, for he was of a great age, and had no children, neither friends, and he feared that he could not of himself escape the waters.

And Morven said to him, soothingly "Lo the people love me, and I will see that thou art saved; for verily thou hast been friendly to me, and done me much service with the king."

And as he thus spake, Morven opened the door of the house and looked forth, and saw that they were quite alone; then he seized the old man by the throat, and ceased not his gripe till he was quite dead. And leaving the body of the elder on the floor, Morven stole from the house and shut the gate. And as he was going to his cave he mused a little while, when, hearing the mighty roar of the waves advancing, and far off the shrieks of women, he lifted up his head, and said, proudly, 'No! in this hour terror alone shall be my slave; I will use no art save the power of my soul." So, leaning on his pine-staff, he strode down to the palace. And it was now evening, and many of the men held torches, that they might see each other's faces in the universal fear. Red flashed the quivering flames on the dark robes and pale front of Morven; and he seemed mightier than the rest, because his face alone was calm amidst the tumult. And louder and hoarser came the roar of the waters; and swift rushed the shades of night over the hastening tide.

And Morven said in a stern voice, "Where is the king; and wherefore is he absent from his people in the hour of dread?" Then the gate of the palace opened, and, behold, Siror was sitting in the hall by the vast pine-fire, and his brother by his side, and his chiefs around him: for they would not deign to come amongst the crowd at the bidding of the herdsman's son.

Then Morven, standing upon a rock above the heads of the people (the same rock whereon he had proclaimed the king), thus spake:—

"Ye desired to know, O sons of Oestrich! wherefore the river hath burst its bounds, and the peril hath come upon you. Learn, then, that the stars resent as the foulest of human crimes an insult to their servants and delegates below. Ye are all aware of the manner of life of Morven, whom ye have surnamed the Prophet! He harms not man nor beast; he lives alone; and, far from the wild joys of the warrior tribe, he worships in awe and fear the Powers of Night. So is he able to advise ye of the coming danger,—so is he able to save ye from the foe. Thus are your huntsmen swift and your warriors bold; and thus do your cattle bring forth their young, and the earth its fruits. What think ye, and what do ye ask to hear? Listen, men of Oestrich!—they have laid snares for my life; and there are amongst you those who have whetted the sword against the bosom that is only filled with love for you all. Therefore have the stern lords of heaven loosened the chains of the river— therefore doth this evil menace ye. Neither will it pass away until they who dug the pit for the servant of the stars are buried in the same."

Then, by the red torches, the faces of the men looked fierce and threatening; and ten thousand voices shouted forth, "Name them who conspired against thy life, O holy prophet! and surely they shall be torn limb from limb."

And Morven turned aside, and they saw that he wept bitterly; and he said,

"Ye have asked me, and I have answered: but now scarce will ye believe the foe that I have provoked against me; and by the heavens themselves I swear, that if my death would satisfy their fury, nor bring down upon yourselves and your children's children, the anger of the throned stars, gladly would I give my bosom to the knife. Yes," he cried, lifting up his voice, and pointing his shadowy arm towards the hall where the king sat by the pine-fire "yes, Siror, the guilty one! take thy sword, and come hither— strike, if thou hast the heart to strike, the Prophet of the Gods!"

The king started to his feet, and the crowd were hushed in a shuddering silence.

Morven resumed:

"Know then, O men of Oestrich! that Siror, and Voltech his brother, and Darvan the elder of the wise men, have purposed to slay your prophet, even at such hour as when alone he seeks the shade of the forest to devise new benefits for you. Let the king deny it, if he can!"

Then Voltoch, of the giant limbs, strode forth from the hall, and his spear quivered in his hand.

"Rightly hast thou spoken, base son of my father's herdsman! and for thy sins shalt thou surely die; for thou liest when thou speakest of thy power with the stars, and thou laughest at the folly of them who hear thee: wherefore put him to death."

Then the chiefs in the hall clashed their arms, and rushed forth to slay the son of Osslah.

But he, stretching his unarmed hands on high, exclaimed, "Hear him, O dread ones of the night!—hark how he blasphemeth!"

Then the crowd took up the word, and cried, "He

blasphemeth—he blasphemeth against the prophet!"

But the king and the chiefs who hated Morven, because of his power with the people, rushed into the crowd; and the crowd were irresolute, nor knew they how to act, for never yet had they rebelled against their chiefs, and they feared alike the prophet and the king.

And Siror cried, "Summon Darvan to us, for he hath watched the steps of Morven, and he shall lift the veil from my people's eyes." Then three of the swift of foot started forth to the house of Darvan.

And Morven cried out with a loud voice, "Hark! thus saith the star who, now riding though yonder cloud, breaks forth upon my eyes—'For the lie that the elder had uttered against my servant, the curse of the stars shall fall upon him.' Seek, and as ye find him so may ye find ever the foes of Morven and the gods!"

A chill and an icy fear fell over the crowd, and even the cheek of Siror grew pale; and Morven, erect and dark above the waving torches, stood motionless with fold arms. And hark—far and fast came on the war-steeds of the wave—the people heard them marching to the land, and tossing their white manes in the roaring wind.

"Lo, as ye listen," said Morven, calmly, "the river sweeps on. Haste, for the gods will have a victim, be it your prophet or your king."

"Slave!" shouted Siror, and his spear left his hand, and far above the heads of the crowd sped hissing beside the dark form of Morven, and rent the trunk of the oak behind. Then the people, wroth at the danger of their beloved seer, uttered a wild yell, and gathered round him with brandished swords, facing their chieftains and their king. But at that instant, ere the war had broken forth among the tribe, the three warriors returned, and they bore Darvan on their shoulders, and laid him at the feet of the king, and they said tremblingly, "Thus found we the elder in the centre of his own hall." And the people saw that Darvan was a corpse, and that the prediction of Morven was thus verified. "So perish the enemies of Morven and the stars!" cried the son of Osslah. And the people echoed the cry. Then the fury of Siror was at its height, and waving his sword above his head he plunged into the crowd, "Thy blood, baseborn, or mine!"

"So be it!" answered Morven, quailing not. "People, smite the blasphemer! Hark how the river pours down upon your children and your hearths! On, on, or ye perish!"

And Siror fell, pierced by five hundred spears.

"Smite! smite!" cried Morven, as the chiefs of the royal house gathered round the king. And the clash of swords, and the gleam of spears, and the cries of the dying, and the yell of the trampling people, mingled with the roar of the elements, and the voices of the rushing wave.

Three hundred of the chiefs perished that night by the swords of their own tribe. And the last cry of the victors was, "Morven the prophet,—*Morven the king!*"

And the son of Osslah, seeing the waves now spreading over the valley, led Orna his wife, and the men of Oestrich, their women, and their children, to a high mount, where they waited the dawning sun. But Orna sat apart and wept bitterly, for her brothers were no more, and her race had perished from the earth. And Morven sought to comfort her in vain.

When the morning rose, they saw that the river had overspread the greater part of the city, and now stayed its course among the hollows of the vale. Then Morven said to the people, "The star-kings are avenged, and their wrath appeased. Tarry only here until the waters have melted into the crevices of the soil." And on the fourth day they returned to the city, and no man dared to name another, save Morven, as the king.

But Morven retired into his cave and mused deeply; and then assembling the people, he gave them new laws; and he made them build a mighty temple in honour of the stars, and made them heap within it all that the tribe held most precious. And he took unto him fifty children from the most famous of the tribe; and he took also ten from among the men who had served him best, and he ordained that they should serve the stars in the great temple: and Morven was their chief. And he put away the crown they pressed upon him, and he chose from among the elders a new king. And he ordained that henceforth the servants only of the stars in the great temple should elect the king and the rulers, and hold council, and proclaim war: but he suffered the king to feast, and to hunt, and to make merry in the banquet-halls. And Morven built altars in the temple, and was the first who, in the North, sacrificed the beast and the bird, and afterwards human flesh, upon the altars. And he drew auguries from the entrails of the victim, and made schools for the science of the prophet; and Morven's piety was the wonder of the tribe, in that he refused to be a king. And Morven the high priest was ten thousand times mightier than the king. He taught the people to till the ground, and to sow the herb; and by his wisdom, and the valour that his prophecies instilled into men, he conquered all the neighbouring tribes. And the sons of Oestrich spread themselves over a mighty empire, and with them spread the name and the laws of Morven. And in every province which he conquered, he ordered them to build a temple to the stars.

But a heavy sorrow fell upon the fears of Morven. The sister of Siror bowed down her head, and survived not long the slaughter of her race. And she left Morven childless. And he mourned bitterly and as one distraught, for her only in the world had his heart the power to love. And he sat down and covered his face, saying:—

"Lo! I have toiled and travailed; and never before in the world did man conquer what I have conquered. Verily the empire of the iron thews and the giant limbs is no more! I have founded a new power, that henceforth shall sway the lands;—the empire of a plotting brain and a commanding mind. But behold! my fate is barren, and I feel already that it will grow neither fruit nor tree as a shelter to mine old age. Desolate and lonely shall I pass unto my grave. O Orna! my beautiful! my loved! none were like unto thee, and to thy love do I owe my glory and my life! Would for thy sake, O sweet bird! that nestled in the dark cavern of my heart,—would for thy sake that thy brethren had been spared, for verily with my life would I have purchased thine. Alas! only when I lost thee did I find that thy love was dearer to me than the fear of others!" And Morven mourned night and day, and none might comfort him.

But from that time forth he gave himself solely up to the cares of his calling; and his nature and his affections, and whatever there was yet left soft in him, grew hard like stone; and he was a man without love, and he forbade love and marriage to the priest.

Now, in his latter years, there arose *other* prophets; for the world had grown wiser even by Morven's wisdom, and some did say unto themselves, "Behold Morven, the herdsman's son, is a king of kings: this did the stars for their servant; shall we not also be servants to the star?"

And they wore black garments like Morven, and went about prophesying of what the stars foretold them. And Morven was exceeding wroth; for he, more than other men, knew that the prophets lied; wherefore he went forth against them with the ministers of the temple, and he took them, and burned them by a slow fire: for thus said Morven to the people:- "A true prophet hath honour, but I only am a true prophet;—to all false prophets there shall be surely death."

And the people applauded the piety of the son of Osslah.

And Morven educated the wisest of the children in the mysteries of the temple, so that they grew up to succeed him worthily.

And he died full of years and honour; and they carved his effigy on a mighty stone before the temple, and the effigy endured for a thousand ages, and whoso looked on it trembled; for the face was calm with the calmness of unspeakable awe!

And Morven was the first mortal of the North that made Religion the stepping-stone to Power. Of a surety Morven was a great man!

It was the last night of the old year, and the stars sat, each upon his ruby throne, and watched with sleepless eyes upon the world. The night was dark and troubled, the dread winds were abroad, and fast and frequent hurried the clouds beneath the thrones of the kings of night. And ever and anon fiery meteors flashed along the depths of heaven, and were again swallowed up in the grave of darkness. But far below his brethren, and with a lurid haze around his orb, sat the discontented star that he watched over the hunters of the North.

And on the lowest abyss of space there was spread a thick and mighty gloom, from which as from a caldron, rose columns of wreathing smoke; and still, when the great winds rested for an instant on their paths, voices of woe and laughter, mingled with shrieks, were heard booming from the abyss to the upper air.

And now, in the middest night, a vast figure rose slowly from the abyss, and its wings threw blackness over the world. High upward to the throne of the discontented star sailed the fearful shape, and the star trembled on his throne when the form stood before him face to face.

And the shape said, "Hail, brother!—all hail!"

"I know thee not," answered the star; "thou art not the archangel that visitest the kings of night."

And the shape laughed loud. "I am the fallen star of the morning!—I am. Lucifer, thy brother! Hast thou not O sullen king! served me and mine? and hast thou not wrested the earth from thy Lord who sittest above, and given it to me, by darkening the souls of men with the religion of fear? Wherefore come, brother, come;— thou hast a throne prepared beside my own in the fiery gloom—

Come! The heavens are no more for thee?"

Then the star rose from his throne, and descended to the side of Lucifer. For ever hath the spirit of discontent had sympathy with the soul of pride. And they sank slowly down to the gulf of gloom.

It was the first night of the new year, and the stars sat each on his ruby throne, and watched with sleepless eyes upon the world. But sorrow dimmed the bright faces of the kings of night, for they mourned in silence and in fear for a fallen brother.

And the gates of the heaven of heavens flew open with a golden sound, and the swift archangel fled down on his silent wings; and the archangel gave to each of the stars, as before, the message of his Lord; and to each star was his appointed charge. And when the heraldry seemed done there came a laugh from the abyss of gloom, and half-way from the gulf rose the lurid shape of Lucifer the fiend!

"Thou countest thy flock ill, O radiant shepherd! Behold! one star is missing from the three thousand and ten!"

"Back to thy gulf, false Lucifer!—the throne of thy brother hath been filled."

And, lo! as the archangel spake, the stars beheld a young and all-lustrous stranger on the throne of the erring star; and his face was so soft to look upon, that the dimmest of human eyes might have gazed upon its splendour unabashed: but the dark fiend alone was dazzled by its lustre, and, with a yell that shook the flaming pillars of the universe, he plunged backward into the gloom.

Then, far and sweet from the arch unseen, came forth the voice of God,—

"Behold! on the throne of the discontented star sits the star of Hope; and he that breathed into mankind the religion of Fear hath a successor in him who shall teach earth the religion of Love!"

And evermore the Star of Fear dwells with Lucifer, and the star of Love keeps vigil in heaven!

THE LIFE OF DREAMS

As they sailed slowly on, Gertrude said, "How like a dream is
ihis sentiment of existence, when, without labour or motion, every
change of scene is brought before us; I am with you, dearest, I do
not feel it less resembling a dream, for I have dreamed of you lately
more than ever. And dreams have become a part of my life itself."

"Speaking of dreams," said Trevylyan, as they pursued that
mysterious subject; "I once during my former residence in Germany
fell in with a singular enthusiast, who had taught himself what he
termed 'A System of Dreaming'. When he first spoke to me upon it I
asked him to explain what he meant, which he did somewhat in the
following words."

"I was born." said he, "with many of the sentiments of the poet,
but without the language to express them; my feelings were
constantly chilled by the intercourse of the actual world—my
family, mere Germans, dull and unimpassioned—had nothing in
common with me; nor did I out of my family find those with whom
I could better sympathise. I was revolted by friendships—for they
were susceptible to every change; I was disappointed in love—for
the truth never approached to my ideal. Nursed early in the lap of
Romance, enamoured of the wild and the adventurous, the
common-places of life were to me inexpressibly tame and joyless.
And yet indolence, which belongs to the poetical character, was
more inviting than that eager and uncontemplative action which
can alone wring enterprise from life. Meditation was my natural
element. I loved to spend the noon reclined by some shady stream,
and in a half sleep to shape images from the glancing sunbeams; a
dim and unreal order of philosophy, that belongs to our nation,
was my favourite intellectual pursuit. And I sought amongst the
Obscure and the Recondite the variety and emotion I could not
find in the Familiar. Thus constantly watching the operations of
the inner-mind, it occurred to me at last that sleep having its own
world, but as yet a rude and fragmentary one, it might be possible
to shape from its chaos all those combinations of beauty, of power,
of glory, and of love, which were denied to me in the world in
which my frame walked and had its being. So soon as this idea
came upon me, I nursed and cherished, and mused over it, till I
found that the imagination began to effect the miracle I desired. By

brooding ardently, intensely, before I retired to rest, over any especial train of thought, over any ideal creations; by keeping the body utterly still and quiescent during the whole day; by shutting out all living adventure, the memory of which might perplex and interfere with the stream of events that I desired to pour forth into the wilds of sleep, I discovered at last that I could lead in dreams a life solely their own, and utterly distinct from the life of day. Towers and palaces, all my heritage and seigneury, rose before me from the depths of night; I quaffed from jewelled cups the Falernian[1] of imperial vaults; music from harps of celestial tone filled up the crevices of air; and the smiles of immortal beauty flushed like sunlight over all. Thus the adventure and the glory that I could not for my waking life obtain, was obtained for me in sleep. I wandered with the gryphon and the gnome; I sounded the horn at enchanted portals; I conquered in the nightly lists; I planted my standard over battlements huge as the painter's Birth of Babylon itself.

"But I was afraid to call forth one shape on whose loveliness to pour all the hidden passion of my soul. I trembled lest my sleep should present me some image which it could never restore, and, waking from which, even the new world I had created might be left desolate for ever. I shuddered lest I should adore a vision which the first ray of morning could smite to the grave.

"In this train of mind I began to ponder whether it might not be possible to connect dreams together; to supply the thread that was wanting; to make one night continue the history of the other, so as to bring together the same shapes and the same scenes, and thus lead a connected and harmonious life, not only in the one half of existence, but in the other, the richer and more glorious, half. No sooner did this idea present itself to me, than I burned to accomplish it. I had before taught myself that Faith is the great creator; that to believe fervently is to make belief true. So I would not suffer my mind to doubt the practicability of its scheme. I shut myself up then entirely by day, refused books, and hated the very sun, and compelled all my thoughts (and sleep is the mirror of thought) to glide in one direction, the direction of my dreams, so that from night to night the imagination might keep up the thread of action, and I might thus lie down full of the past dream and confident of the sequel. Not for one day only, or for one month, did I pursue this system, but I continued it zealously and sternly till at length it began to succeed. "Who shall tell," cried the enthusiast,— I see him now with his deep, bright, sunken eyes, and his wild hair thrown backward from his brow, "the rapture I experience, when first, faintly and half distinct, I perceived the harmony I had invoked dawn upon my dreams?" At first there was only a partial and desultory connexion between them; my eye recognised certain shapes, my ear certain tones common to each; by degrees these augmented in number, and were more defined in outline. At length one fair face broke forth from among the ruder forms, and night after night appeared mixing with them for a moment and then vanishing, just as the mariner watches, in a clouded sky, the moon shining through the drifting rack, and quickly gone. My curiosity was now vividly excited, the face, with its lustrous eyes, and seraph features, roused all the emotions that no living shape had called forth. I became enamoured of a dream, and as the statue to the Cyprian[2] was my creation to me; so from this intent and unceasing passion, I at length worked out my reward. My dream became more palpable; I spoke with it; I knelt to it; my lips were pressed to its own; we exchanged the vows of love, and morning only separated us with the certainty that at night we should meet again. "Thus then," continued my visionary, "I commenced a history utterly separate from the history of the world, and it went on alternatively with my harsh and chilling history of the day, equally regular and equally continuous. And what, you ask, was that history? Me thought I was a prince in some Eastern island, that had no features in common with the colder north of my native home. By day I looked upon the dull walls of a German town, and saw homely or squalid forms passing before me; the sky was dim and the sun cheerless. Night came on with her thousand stars, and brought me the dews of sleep. Then suddenly there was a new world; the richest fruits hung from the trees in cluster of gold and purple. Palaces of the quaint fashion of the sunnier climes, with spiral minarets and glittering cupolas, were mirrored upon vast lakes sheltered by the palm-tree and banana. The sun seemed a different orb, so mellow and gorgeous were his beams; birds and winged things of all hues fluttered in the shining air; the faces and garments of men were not of the northern regions of the world, and their voices spoke a tongue which, strange at first, by degrees I interpreted. Sometimes I made war upon neighbouring kings; sometimes I chased the spotted pard through the vast gloom of immemorial forests; my life was at once a life of enterprise and pomp. But above all there was the history of my love! I thought there were a thousand difficulties in the way of attaining its possession. Many were the rocks I had to scale, and the battles to wage, and the fortresses to storm, in order to win her as my bride. But at last," (continued the enthusiast) "she is won, she is my own! Time in that wild world, which I visit nightly, passes not so slowly as in this, and yet an hour may be the same as a year. This continuity of existence, this successive series of dreams, so different from the broken incoherence of other men's sleep, at times bewilders me with strange and suspicious thoughts. What if this glorious sleep be a real life, and this dull waking the true repose? Why not? What is there more faithful in the one than in the other? And there have I garnered and collected all of pleasure that I am capable of feeling. I seek no joy in this world—I form no ties, I feast not, nor love, nor make merry—I am only impatient till the hour when I may re-enter my royal realms and pour my renewed delight into the bosom of my bright Ideal. There then have I found all that the world denied me; there have I realised the yearning and the inspiration within me; there have I coined the untold poetry into the Felt—the Seen!"

I found, continued Trevylyan[3], that his tale was corroborated by inquiry into the visionary's habits. He shunned society; avoided all unnecessary movement or excitement. He fared with rigid abstemiousness, and only appeared to feel pleasure as the day departed, and the hour of return to his imaginary kingdom approached. He always retired to rest punctually at a certain hour, and would sleep so soundly, that a cannon fired under his window would not arouse him. He never, which may seem singular, spoke or moved much in his sleep, but was peculiarly calm, almost to the appearance of lifelessness; but, discovering once that he had been watched in sleep, he was wont afterwards carefully to secure the chamber from intrusion. His victory over the natural incoherence of sleep had, when I first knew him, lasted for some years; possibly what imagination first produced was afterward continued by habit.

I saw him again a few months subsequent to this confession, and he seemed to me much changed. His health was broken, and his abstraction had deepened into gloom.

I questioned him of the cause of the alteration, and he answered me with great reluctance—

"She is dead," said he; "my realms are desolate! A serpent stung her, and she died in those very arms. Vainly, when I started from my sleep in horror and despair, vainly did I say to myself,— This is but a dream. I shall see her again. A vision cannot die! Hath it flesh that decays? is it not a spirit—bodiless—indissoluble? With what terrible anxiety I awaited the night! Again I slept, and the DREAM lay again before me—dead and withered. Even the ideal can vanish. I assisted in the burial; I laid her in the earth; I heaped the monumental mockery over her form. And never since hath she, or aught like her, revisited my dreams. I see her only when I wake; thus to wake is indeed to dream! But," continued the visionary in a solemn voice, "I feel myself departing from this world, and with a fearful joy; for I think there may be a land beyond even the land of sleep, where I shall see her again,—a land in which a vision itself may be restored."

And in truth, concluded Trevylyan, the dreamer died shortly afterwards, suddenly, and in his sleep. And never before, perhaps, had Fate so literally made a living man (with his passions and his powers, his ambition and his love) the plaything and puppet of a dream!

"Ah," said Vane, who had heard the latter part of Trevylyan's story; "could the German have bequeathed to us his secret, what a refuge should we possess from the ills of earth! The dungeon and disease, poverty, affliction, shame, would cease to be the tyrants of our lot; and to Sleep we should confine our history and transfer our emotions."

"Gertrude," whispered the lover, "what his kingdom and his bride were to the Dreamer, art thou to me!"

ARASMANES; or The Seeker

In the broad plains of Chaldæa[1], and not the least illustrious of those shepherd-sages from whom came our first learning of the lights of heaven, the venerable Chosphor saw his age decline into the grave. Upon his death-bed he thus addressed his only son, the young Arasmanes, in whose piety he recognised, even in that gloomy hour, a consolation and a blessing; and for whose growing renown for wisdom and for valour, the faint pulses of expiring life yet beat with paternal pride.

"Arasmanes," said he, "I am about to impart to you the only secret which, after devoting eighty years to unravel the many mysteries of knowledge, I consider worthy of transmitting to my child. Thou knowest that I have wandered over the distant regions of the world, and have experienced, with all the vicissitudes, some of the triumphs, and many of the pleasures, of life. Learn, from my experience, that earth possesses nothing which can reward the pursuit, or satisfy the desire. When you see the stars shining down upon the waters, you behold an image of the visionary splendours of hope: the light sparkles on the wave; but it neither warms while it glitters, nor can it, for a single instant, arrest the progress of the stream from the dark gulf into which it hastens to merge itself and be lost. It was not till my old age that this conviction grew upon my mind; and about that time I discovered, from one of the sacred books to which my studies were then applied, the secret I am now about to confide to thy ear. Know, my son, that in the extremities of Asia there is a garden in which the God of the Universe placed the first parents of mankind. In that garden the sun never sets; nor does the beauty of the seasons wane. *There*, is neither Ambition, nor Avarice, nor False Hope, nor its child, Regret. *There*, is neither age nor deformity; diseases are banished from the air; eternal youth, and the serenity of an unbroken happiness, are the prerogative of all things that breathe therein. For a mystic and unknown sin our first parents were banished from this happy clime, and their children scattered over the earth. Super-human beings are placed at its portals, and clouds and darkness veil it from the eyes of ordinary men. But, to the virtuous and to the bold, there is no banishment from the presence of God; and by them the darkness may be penetrated, the dread guardians softened, and the portals of the divine land be passed. Thither, then, my son—

early persuaded that the rest of earth is paved with sorrow and with care—thither, then bend thy adventurous way. Fain could I have wished that, in my stronger manhood, when my limbs could have served my will, I had learned this holy secret, and repaired in search of the ancestral clime. Avail thyself of my knowledge; and, in the hope of thy happiness, I shall die contented." The pious son pressed the hand of his sire, and promised obedience to his last command.

"But, oh, my father!" said he, "how shall I know in what direction to steer my course? To this land, who shall be my guide, or what my clue? Can ship, built by mortal hands, anchor at its coast; or can we say to the camel-driver, 'Thou art approaching to the goal?'"

The old man pointed to the east.

"From the east," said he, "dawns the sun—emblem of the progress of the mind's light; from the east comes all of science that we know. Born in its sultry regions, seek only to pierce to its extreme; and guiding thyself by the stars of heaven ever in one course, reach at last the ADEN that shall reward thy toils."

And Chosphor died, and was buried with his fathers.

After a short interval of mourning, Arasmanes took leave of his friends: and, turning his footsteps to the east, sought the gates of paradise.

He travelled far, and alone, for several weeks; and the stars were his only guides. By degrees, as he advanced, he found that the existence of Aden was more and more acknowledged. Accustomed from his boyhood to the companionship of sages, it was their abodes that he sought in each town or encampment through which he passed. By them his ardour was confirmed; for they all agreed in the dim and remote tradition of some beautiful region in the farthest east, from which the existing races of the earth were banished, and which was jealously guarded from profane approach by the wings of the spirits of God. But, if he communicated to any one his daring design, he had the mortification to meet only the smile of derision, or the incredulous gaze of wonder: by some he was thought a madman, and by others an impostor. So that, at last, he prudently refrained from revealing his intentions, and contented himself with seeking the knowledge, and listening to the conjectures of others.

At length the traveller emerged from a mighty forest, through which, for several days, he had threaded his weary way; and beautiful beyond thought was the landscape that broke upon his view. A plain covered with the richest verdure lay before him; through the trees that, here and there, darkened over the emerald ground, were cut alleys, above which hung festoons of many-coloured flowers, whose hues sparkled amidst the glossy foliage, and whose sweets steeped the air as with a bath. A stream, clear as crystal, flowed over golden sands, and wherever the sward was greenest, gathered itself into delicious fountains, and sent upwards its dazzling spray, as if to catch the embraces of the sun, whose beams kissed it in delight.

The wanderer paused in ecstasy; a sense of luxurious rapture, which he had never before experienced, crept into his soul. "Behold!" murmured he, "my task is already done; and Aden, the land of happiness and of youth, lies before me!"

While he thus spake, a sweet voice answered—"Yes, O happy stranger!—thy task is done: this is the land of happiness and of youth!"

He turned, and a maiden of dazzling beauty was by his side. "Enjoy the present," said she, "and so wilt thou defy the future. Ere yet the world was, Love brooded over the unformed shell, till from beneath the shadow of his wings burst forth the life of the young creation. Love, then is the true God, and who so serveth him he admits into the mysteries of a temple erected before the stars. Behold! thou enterest now upon the threshold of the temple; thou art in the land of happiness and youth!"

Enchanted with these words, Arasmanes gave himself up to the sweet intoxication they produced upon his soul. He suffered the nymph to lead him deeper into the valley; and now, from a thousand vistas in the wood, trooped forth beings, some of fantastic, some of the most harmonious, shapes. There, were the satyr and the faun[2], and the youthful Bacchus—mixed with the multiform deities of India, and the wild objects of Egyptian worship; but more numerous than all were the choral nymphs, that spiritualized the reality, by incorporating the dreams, of beauty; and, wherever he looked, one laughing Face seemed to peer forth from the glossy leaves, and to shed, as from its own joyous yet tender aspect, a tenderness and a joy over all things; and he asked how this Being, that seemed to have the power of multiplying itself everywhere, was called?—And its name was Eros.

For a time the length of which he knew not—for in that land no measurement of time was kept—Arasmanes was fully persuaded that it was Aden to which he had attained. He felt his youth as if it were something palpable; everything was new to him—even in the shape of the leaves, and the whisper of the odorous airs, he found wherewithal to marvel at and admire. Enamoured of the maiden that had first addressed him, at her slightest wish (and she was full of all beautiful caprices), he was ready to explore even the obscurest recess of the valley which now appeared to him unbounded. He never wearied of a single hour. He felt as if weariness were impossible; and, with every instant, he repeated to himself, "In the land of happiness and youth I am a dweller."

One day, as he was conversing with his beloved, and gazing upon her face, he was amazed to behold that, since the last time he had gazed upon it, a wrinkle had planted itself upon the ivory surface of her brow; and, even while half doubting the evidence of his eyes, new wrinkles seemed slowly to form over the forehead, and the transparent roses of her cheek to wane and fade! He concealed, as well as he could, the mortification and wonder that he experienced at this strange phenomenon; and, no longer daring to gaze upon a face from which before he had drunk delight as from a fountain, he sought excuses to separate himself from her, and wandered, confused and bewildered with his own thoughts, into the wood. The fauns, and the dryads, and the youthful face of Bacchus, and the laughing aspect of Eros, came athwart him from time to time; yet the wonder that had clothed them with fascination was dulled within his breast. Nay, he thought the poor wine-god had a certain vulgarity in his air, and he felt an angry impatience at the perpetual gaiety of Eros.

And now, whenever he met his favourite nymph—who was as the queen of the valley—he had the chagrin to perceive that the wrinkles deepened with every time; youth seemed rapidly to desert her; and instead of a maiden scarcely escaped from childhood, it was an old coquette that he had been so desperately in love with.

One day he could not resist saying to her, though with some embarrassment—

"Pray, dearest, is it many years since you have inhabited this valley?"

"Oh, indeed, many!" said she, smiling.

"You are not, then, very young?" rejoined Arasmanes, ungallantly.

"What!" cried the nymph, changing colour—"Do you begin to discover age in my countenance? Has any wrinkle yet appeared

85

upon my brow? You are silent. Oh, cruel Fate! will you not spare even this lover?" And the poor nymph burst into tears.

"My dear love," said Arasmanes, painfully, "it is true that time begins to creep upon you, but my friendship shall be eternal."

Scarcely had he uttered these words, when the nymph, rising, fixed upon him a long, sorrowful look, and, then, with a loud cry, vanished from his sight. Thick darkness, as a veil, fell over the plains; the NOVELTY of life, with its attendant, POETRY, was gone from the wanderer's path for ever.

A sudden sleep crept over his senses. He awoke confused and unrefreshed, and a long and gradual ascent, but over mountains green indeed, and watered by many streams gushing from the heights, stretched before him. Of the valley he had mistaken for Aden not a vestige remained. He was once more on the real and solid earth.

For several days, discontented and unhappy, the young adventurer pursued his course, still seeking only the east, and still endeavouring to console himself for the sweet delusions of the past by hoping an Aden in the future.

The evening was still and clear; the twilight star broke forth over those giant plains—free from the culture and the homes of men, which yet make the character of the eastern and the earlier world; a narrow stream, emerging from a fissure in a small rock covered with moss, sparkled forth under the light of the solemn heavens, and flowed far away, till lost amongst the gloom of a forest of palms. By the source of this stream sat an aged man and a young female. And the old man was pouring into his daughter's ear—for Azraaph held to Ochtor that holy relationship—the first doctrines of the world's wisdom; those wild but lofty conjectures by which philosophy penetrated into the nature and attributes of God; and reverently the young maiden listened, and meekly shone down the star of eve upon the dark yet lustrous beauty of her earnest countenance.

It was at this moment that a stranger was seen descending from the hills that bordered the mighty plains; and he, too, worn and tired with long travel, came to the stream to refresh his burning thirst, and lave the dust from his brow.

He was not at first aware of the presence of the old man and the maiden; for they were half concealed beneath the shadow of the rock from which the stream flowed. But the old man, who was one of those early hermits with whom wisdom was the child of solitude, and who weary with a warring and savage world, had long since retired to a cavern not far from the source of that stream, and dwelt apart with Nature—the memories of a troubled Past, and the contemplation of a mysterious Future,—the old man, I say, accustomed to proffer to the few wanderers that from time to time descended the hills (seeking the cities of the east) the hospitalities of food and shelter, was the first to break the silence.

Arasmanes accepted with thankfulness the offers of the hermit, and that night he became Ochtor's guest. There were many chambers in the cavern, hollowed either by the hand of Nature, or by some early hunters on the hill; and into one of these the old man, after the Chaldæan had refreshed himself with the simple viands of the hermitage, conducted the wanderer: it was covered with dried and fragrant mosses; and the sleep of Arasmanes was long, and he dreamed many cheerful dreams.

When he arose the next morning he found his entertainers were not within the cavern. He looked forth, and beheld them once more by the source of the stream, on which the morning sun shone, and round which fluttered the happy wings of the desert birds. The wanderer sought his hosts in a spot on which they were accustomed, morning and eve, to address the Deity. "Thou dost not purpose to leave us soon," said the hermit; "for he who descends from yon mountains must have traversed a toilsome way, and his limbs will require rest."

Arasmanes, gazing on the beauty of Azraaph, answered, "In truth, did I not fear that I should disturb thy reverent meditations, the cool of thy plains and quiet of thy cavern, and, more than all, thy converse and kind looks, would persuade me, my father, to remain with thee many days."

"Behold how the wandering birds give life and merriment to the silent stream!" said the sage; "and so to the solitary man are the footsteps of his kind." And Arasmanes sojourned with Ochtor the old man.

"THIS, then is thy tale," said Ochtor; "and thou still believest in the visionary Aden of thy father's dreams. Doubtless such a land existed once for our happier sires; or why does tradition preserve it to the race that behold it not? But the shadow wraps it, and the angel guards. Waste not thy life in a pursuit, without a clue, for a goal that thou never mayest attain. Lose not the charm of earth in seeking after the joys of Aden. Tarry with us, my son, in these still retreats. This is the real Aden of which thy father spake; for here comes neither passion nor care. The mortifications and the disappointments of earth fall not upon the recluse. Behold, my daughter hath found favour in thine eyes—she loveth thee—she is beautiful and tender of heart. Tarry with us, my son, and forget the lessons that thy sire, weary with a world which he yet never had the courage to quit, gave thee from the false wisdom of Discontent."

"Thou art right, venerable Ochtor," cried Arasmanes with enthusiasm; "give me but thy daughter, and I will ask for no other Aden than these plains."

The sun had six times renewed his course, and Arasmanes still dwelt in the cave of Ochtor. In the fair face of Azraaph he discovered no wrinkles—her innocent love did not pall upon him; the majestic calm of Nature breathed its own tranquillity into his soul, and in the lessons of Ochtor he took a holy delight. He found in his wisdom that which at once stilled the passions and inspired the thoughts. At times, however, and of late more frequently than ever, strong yearnings after the Aden he had so vainly pursued were yet felt. He felt that curse of monotony which is the invariable offspring of quiet.

At the end of the sixth year, as one morning they stood without the door of the cavern, and their herds fed tranquilly around them, a band of men from the western hills came suddenly in view: they were discovered before they had time to consider whether they should conceal themselves; they had no cause, however, for fear—the strangers were desirous only of food and rest.

Foremost of this band was an aged man of majestic mien, and clothed in the richest garments of the east. Loose flowed his purple robe, and bright shone the jewels on the girdle that clasped this sword. As he advanced to accost Ochtor, upon the countenance of each of the old men grew doubt, astonishment, recognition, and joy. "My brother!" burst from the lips of both, and the old chief fell upon Ochtor's bosom and wept aloud. The brothers remained alone the whole day, and at nightfall they parted with many tears; and Zamielides, the son of the chief (who was with the band), knelt to Ochtor, and Ochtor blessed him.

Now, when all were gone, and Silence once more slept upon the plains, Ochtor went forth alone, and Azraaph said unto her husband, "My father's mind seems disquieted and sad; go forth, I pray thee, my beloved, and comfort him; the dews lie thick upon the grass, and my father is very old."

By the banks of the stream stood Ochtor, and his arms were folded on his breast; the river-horses were heard snorting in the distance, and the wild zebras came to drink at the wave; and the presence of the beasts made more impressive the solitude of the old man.

"Why art thou disquieted, my father?" said Arasmanes.

"Have I not parted with my near of kin?"

"But thou didst never hope to meet them; and are not thy children left thee?"

Ochtor waved his hand with an unwonted impatience.

"Listen to me, Arasmanes. Know that Zamiel and I were brothers. Young and ardent, each of us aspired to rule our kind, and each of us imagined he had the qualities that secure command; but mark, *my* arm was the stronger in the field, and *my* brain was the subtler in the council. We toiled and schemed, and rose into repute among our tribe, but Envy was busy with our names. Our herds were seized—we were stripped of our rank—we were degraded to the level of our slaves. Then, disgusted with my race, I left their cities, and in these vast solitudes I forgot ambition in content. But my brother was of more hopeful heart; with a patient brow he veiled the anger he endured. Lo, he hath been rewarded! His hour came—he gathered together his friends in secret—he smote our enemies in the dead of night; and at morning, behold, he was hailed chieftain of the tribe. This night he rides with his son to the king of the City of Golden Palaces, whose daughter that son is about to wed. Had I not weakly renounced my tribe—had I not fled hither, that glorious destiny would have been mine; *I* should have been the monarch of my race, and my daughter have matched with kings. Marvellest thou, now, that I am disquieted, or that my heart is sore within me?"

And Arasmanes saw that the sage had been superior to the world, only while he was sickened of the world.

And Ochtor nourished the discontent he had formed to his dying day; and, within three months from that night, Arasmanes buried him by the source of the solitary stream.

The death of Ochtor, and his previous confession, deeply affected Arasmanes. He woke as from a long sleep. Solitude had lost its spell; and he perceived that inactivity itself may be the parent of remorse. "If," thought he, "so wise, so profound a mind as that of Ochtor was thus sensible to the memories of ambition— if, on the verge of death, he thus regretted the solitude in which he had buried his years, and felt, upon the first tidings from the great world, that he had wasted the promise and powers of life, how much more accessible should *I* be to such feelings, in the vigour of manhood, and with the one great object which I swore to my father to pursue, unattained, and scarcely attempted? Surely it becomes me to lose no longer time in these houseless wastes; but to rise and gird up my loins, and seek with Azraaph, my wife, for that Aden which we will enter together!"

These thoughts soon ripened into resolve; and not the less so in that, Ochtor being dead, Arasmanes had now no companion for his loftier and more earnest thoughts. Azraaph was beautiful and gentle; but the moment he began to talk about the stars, she unaffectedly yawned in his face. She was quite contented with the solitude, for she knew of no other world; and the herds and the streamlet, and every old bush around the cavern, were society to her; but her content, as Arasmanes began to discover, was that of ignorance, and not of wisdom.

Azraaph wept bitterly on leaving the cavern; but by degrees as they travelled slowly on, the novelty of what they saw reconciled her to change; and, except at night, when she was weary of spirit, she ceased to utter her regrets for the stream and the quiet cave. They travelled eastward for several weeks, and met with no living thing by the way, save a few serpents, and a troop of wild horses. At length one evening, they found themselves in the suburbs of a splendid city. As they approached the gates they drew back, dazzled with the lustre, for the gates were of burnished gold, which shone bright and glittering as they caught a sunny light from the lamps of naphtha that hung frequent, from the mighty walls.

They inquired, as they passed the gates, the name of the city; and they heard with some surprise, and more joy, that it was termed, "The City of Golden Palaces."

"Here, then," cried Azraaph, "we shall be well received; for the son of my father's brother is wedded to the daughter of the king."

"And here, then, will be many sages," thought Arasmanes, "who will doubtless, have some knowledge of the true situation of Aden."

They were much struck, as they proceeded through the streets, with the bustle, and life, and animation, that reigned around, even at that late hour. With the simplicity natural to persons who had lived so long in a desert, they inquired at once for the king's palace. The first time Arasmanes asked the question, it was of a young lord, who, very sumptuously dressed, was treading the streets with great care, lest he should soil the hem of his robe. The young lord looked at him with grave surprise, and passed on. The next person he asked was a rude boor, who was carrying a bundle of wood on his shoulders. The boor laughed in his face; and Arasmanes, indignant at the insult, struck him to the ground. There then came by a judge, and Arasmanes asked him the same question.

"The king's palace!" said the judge; "and what want ye with the king's palace?"

"Behold, the daughter of the king is married to my wife's cousin."

"Thy wife's cousin! Thou art mad to say it; yet stay, thou lookest poor, friend" (here the judge frowned terribly). "Thy garments are scanty and worn. I fancy thou hast neither silver nor gold."

"Thou sayest right," replied Arasmanes; "I have neither."

"Ho, ho!" quoth the judge; "he confesses his guilt; he owns that he has neither silver nor gold. Here, soldiers, seize this man and woman. Away with them to prison; and let them be brought up for sentence of death to-morrow. We will then decide whether they shall be hanged or starved. The wretches have, positively, neither silver nor gold; and, what is worse, they own it!"

"Is it possible!" cried the crowd; and a shudder of horror crept through the by-standers. "Away with them!—away with them! Long life to Judge Kaly, whose eye never sleeps, and who preserves us for ever from the poor!"

The judge walked on, shedding tears of virtuous delight at the reputation he had acquired.

Arasmanes and Azraaph were hurried off to prison, where Azraaph cried herself to sleep, and Arasmanes, with folded arms and downcast head, indulged his meditations on the very extraordinary notions of crime that seemed common to the sons of the City of Golden Palaces. They were disturbed the next morning by loud shouts beneath the windows of the prison. Nothing could equal the clamour that they heard; but it seemed the clamour of joy. In fact, that morning the princess who had married Azraaph's cousin had been safely brought to bed of her first child; and great was the joy and the noise throughout the city. Now, it was the custom of that country, whenever any one of the royal family was pleased to augment the population of the world, for the father of the child to go round to all the prisons in the city, and release the prisoners. What good fortune of Arasmanes and Azraaph, that the princess had been brought to bed before they were hanged!

And, by-and-by, amidst cymbal and psalter, with banners above him and spears around, came the young father to the gaol, in which our unfortunate couple were confined.

"Have you any extraordinary criminals in your prison?" asked the prince, of the head gaoler: for he was studying at that time, to be affable.

"Only one man, my lord, who was committed last night; and who absolutely confessed in cold blood, and without torture, that he had neither silver nor gold. It is a thousand pities that such a miscreant should be suffered to go free!"

"You are right," said the prince; "and what impudence to confess his guilt! I should like to see so remarkable a criminal."

So saying, the prince dismounted, and followed the gaoler to the cell in which Arasmanes and his wife were confined. They recognised their relation at once; for, in that early age of the world, people in trouble had a wonderfully quick memory in recollecting relatives in power. Azraaph ran to throw herself on the prince's neck (which the guards quickly prevented), and the stately Arasmanes began to utter his manly thanks for the visit.

"These people are mad," cried the prince hastily. "Release them; but let me escape first." So saying, he ran down stairs so fast that he nearly broke his neck; and then, mounting his horse, pursued his way to the other prisons, amidst the shouts of the people.

Arasmanes and Azraaph were now turned out into the streets. They were exceedingly hungry; and they went into the first baker's shop they saw, and asked the rites of hospitality.

"Certainly; but your money first," said the baker.

Arasmanes, made wise by experience, took care not to reply that he had no money; "But," said he, "I have left it behind me at my lodging. Give me the bread now, and lo, I will repay thee to-morrow."

"Very well," said the baker; "but that sword of yours has a handsome hilt: leave it with me till you return with the monies."

So Arasmanes took the bread, and left the sword.

They were not refreshed, and resolved to hasten from so

dangerous a city, when, just as they turned into a narrow street, they were suddenly seized by six soldiers, blindfolded, gagged, and hurried away, whither they knew not. At last they found themselves ascending a flight of stairs. A few moments more, and the bandages were removed from their mouths and eyes, and they saw themselves in a gorgeous chamber, and alone in the presence of the prince, their cousin.

He embraced them tenderly. "Forgive me," said he, "for appearing to forget you; but it was as much as my reputation was worth in this city to acknowledge relations who confessed to have neither silver nor gold. By the beard of my grandfather, how could you be so imprudent? Do you not know that you are in a country in which the people worship only one deity—the god of the precious metals? Not to have the precious metals is not to have virtue; to confess it, is to be an atheist. No power could have saved you from death, either by hanging or starvation, if the princess, my wife, had not been luckily brought to bed to-day."

"What a strange—what a barbarous country!" said Arasmanes.

"Barbarous!" echoed the prince; "this is the most civilised people in the world,—nay, the whole world acknowledges it. In no country are the people so rich, and, therefore, so happy. For those who have no money it is, indeed, a bad place of residence; for those who have, it is the land of happiness itself. Yes, it is the true Aden."

"Aden! What then, you, too, have heard of Aden?"

"Surely! and this is it—the land of freedom—of happiness—of gold!" cried the prince, with enthusiasm: "remain with us and see."

"Without doubt," thought Arasmanes, "this country lies in the far east; it has received me inhospitably at first; but perhaps the danger I escaped was but the type and allegorical truth of the sworded angel of which tradition hath spoken." "But," said he, aloud, "I have no gold, and no silver, O my prince!"

"Heed not that," answered the kind Zamielides: "I have enough for all. You shall be provided for this very day."

"But will not the people recognise me as the poor stranger?"

The prince laughed for several minutes so loudly that they feared he was going into fits.

"What manner of man art thou, Arasmanes?" said he, when he was composed enough to answer; "the people of this city never know what a man has been when he is once rich? Appear to-morrow in purple, and they will never dream that they saw thee yesterday in rags."

The kind Zamielides, then, conducting his cousins into his own chamber, left them to attire themselves in splendid garments, which he had ordered to be prepared for them. He gave them a palace and large warehouses of merchandise.

"Behold," said he, taking Arasmanes to the top of a mighty tower which overlooked the sea,—"behold yonder ships that rise like a forest of masts from that spacious harbour; the six vessels with the green flags are thine. I will teach thee the mysteries of Trade, and thou wilt soon be as wealthy as myself."

"And what is Trade, my lord?" said Arasmanes.

"It is the worship that the people of this country pay to their god," answered the prince.

Arasmanes was universally courted; so wise, so charming a person had never appeared in the City of Golden Palaces; and as to the beauty of Azraaph, it was declared the very masterpiece of Nature. Intoxicated with the homage they received, and the splendour in which they lived, their days glided on in a round of luxurious enjoyment.

"Right art thou, O Zamielides!" cried Arasmanes, as his ships returned with new treasure; "the City of Golden Palaces is the true Aden."

Arasmanes had now been three years in the city; and you might perceive that a great change had come over his person: the hues of health had faded from his cheeks: his brow was care-worn—his step slow—his lips compressed. He no longer thought that he lived in the true Aden; and yet for Aden itself he would scarcely have quitted the City of Golden Palaces. Occupied solely with the task of making and spending money, he was consumed with the perpetual fear of losing, and the perpetual anxiety to increase his stock. He trembled at every darker cloud that swept over the heavens; he turned pale at every ruder billow that agitated the sea. He lived a life of splendid care: and the pleasures which relieved it were wearisome because of their sameness. He saw but little of his once idolised Azraaph. Her pursuits divided her from him. In so civilised a country they could not be always together. If he spoke of his ships, he wearied her to death; if she spoke of the festivals she had adorned, he was equally tired of the account.

The court was plunged in grief. Zamielides was seized with a fever. All the wise men attended him; but he turned his face to the wall and died. Arasmanes mourned for him more sincerely than any one; for, besides that Arasmanes had great cause to be grateful

94

to him, he knew, also, that if any accident happened to his vessels, he had now no friend willing to supply the loss. This made him more anxious than ever about the safety of his wealth. A year after this event, the new king of the City of Golden Palaces thought fit to go to war. The war lasted four years; and two millions of men were killed on all sides. The second year Arasmanes was at a splendid banquet given at the court. A messenger arrived, panting and breathless. A great battle at sea had been fought. Ten thousand of the king's subjects had been killed.

"But who won the battle?" cried the king.

"Your majesty."

The air was rent with shouts of joy.

"One little accident only," continued the herald, "happened the next day. Three of the scattered war ships of the enemy fell in with the vessels of some of our merchants returning from Ophir, laden with treasure, and, in revenge, they burned and sunk them."

"Were my ships of the number?" asked Arasmanes, with faltering tongue.

"It was of thy ships that I spoke," answered the messenger.

But nobody thought of Arasmanes, or of the ten thousand subjects that were killed. The city was out of its wits with joy that his majesty had won the victory.

"Alas! I am a ruined man!" said Arasmanes, as he sat with ashes on his head.

"And we can give no more banquets," sighed his wife.

"And everybody will trample upon us," said Arasmanes.

"And we must give up our palace," groaned the tender Azraaph.

"But one ship remains to me!" cried Arasmanes, starting up; "it is now in port. I will be its captain. I will sail myself with it to Ophir. I will save my fortunes, or perish in the attempt."

"And I will accompany thee, my beloved," exclaimed Azraaph, flinging herself on his neck; "*for* I cannot bear the pity of the wives whom I have outshone!"

The sea was calm, and the wind favourable when the unfortunate pair entered their last ship; and, for a whole week, the gossip at court was of the folly of Arasmanes, and the devotion of his wife.

They had not been many weeks at sea, before an adverse wind set in, which drove them out of their destined course. They were beaten eastward, and, at length, even the oldest and most experienced of the mariners confessed they had entered seas utterly unknown to them. Worn and wearied, when their water was just out, and their provisions exhausted, they espied land, and, at nightfall the ship anchored on a green and pleasant shore. The inhabitants, half-naked, and scarce escaped from the first savage state of nature, ran forth to meet and succour them: by mighty fires the seamen dried their wet garments, and forgot the hardships they had endured. They remained several days with the hospitable savages, repaired their vessel, and replenished its stores. But what especially attracted the notice of Arasmanes, was the sight of some precious diamonds which, in a rude crown, the chief of the savages wore on his head. He learned from signs easy of interpretation, that these diamonds abounded in a certain island in the farthest east; and that from time to time large fragments of rock in which they were imbedded were cast upon the shore. But when Arasmanes signified his intention to seek this island, the savages, by gestures of horror and dismay, endeavoured to denote the dangers that attended the enterprise, and to dissuade him from attempting it. Naturally bold, and consumed with his thirst for wealth, these signs made but little impression upon the Chaldæan; and one fair morning he renewed his voyage. Steering perpetually towards the east, and with favouring winds, they came, on the tenth day, in sight of an enormous rock, which shone far down over the waters with so resplendent a glory, as to dazzle the eyes of the seamen. Diamond and ruby, emerald and carbuncle, glittered from the dark soil of the rock, and promised to the heart of the humblest mariner the assurance of illimitable wealth. Never was human joy more ecstatic than that of the crew as the ship neared the coast. The sea was in this place narrow and confined, the opposite shore was also in view—black, rugged, and herbless, with pointed rocks, round which the waves sent their white foam on high, guarding its drear approach: little recked they, however, of the opposite shore, as their eyes strained towards "The Island of Precious Stones." They were in the middle of the strait, when suddenly the waters became agitated and convulsed; the vessel rocked to and fro; something glittering appeared beneath the surface; and at length, they distinctly perceived the scales and tail of an enormous serpent.

Thereupon a sudden horror seized the whole crew; they recognised the truth of that tradition known to all seamen, that in the farthest east lived the vast Snake of the Ocean, whose home no vessel ever approached without destruction. All thought of the diamond rock faded from their souls. They fell at once upon their knees, and poured forth unconscious prayers. But high above all rose the tall form of Arasmanes: little cared he for serpent or tradition. Fame, and fortune, and life, were set upon one cast. "Rouse thee!" said he, spurning the pilot, "or we drive upon the opposite shore. Behold, the island of inexhaustible wealth glows upon us!"

Scarce had the words left his lips, when, with a slow and fearful hiss, the serpent of the eastern seas[3] reared his head from the ocean. Dark and huge as the vastest cavern in which ghoul or Afrite ever dwelt was the abyss of his jaws, and the lurid and terrible eyes outshone even the lustre of the diamond rock.

"I defy thee!" cried Arasmanes, waving his sword above his head; when suddenly the ship whirled round and round; the bold Chaldæan was thrown with violence on the deck, he felt the waters whirl and blacken over him: and then all sense of life deserted him.

When he came to himself, Arasmanes was lying on the hot sands of the shore opposite to the Diamond Isle; wrecks of the vessel were strewn around him, and here and there the dead bodies of his seamen. But at his feet lay, swollen and distorted, the shape of his beautiful Azraaph, the sea-weeds twisted round her limbs, and the deformed shell-fish crawling over her long hair. And tears crept into the eyes of the Chaldæan, and all his old love for Azraaph returned, and he threw himself down beside her mangled remains, and tore his hair; the schemes of the later years were swept away from his memory like visions, and he remembered only the lone cavern and his adoring bride.

Time rolled on, and Azraaph was buried in the sands; Arasmanes tore himself from the solitary grave, and, striking into the interior of the coast, sought once more to discover the abodes of men. He travelled far and beneath burning suns, and at night he surrounded his resting-places with a circle of fire, for the wild beasts and the mighty serpents were abroad: scant and unwholesome was the food he gleaned from the berries and rank roots that now and then were visible in the drear wastes through which he passed; and in this course of hardship and travail he held commune with his own heart. He felt as if cured for ever of the evil passions. Avarice seemed gone from his breast, and he dreamed that no unholy desire could succeed to its shattered throne.

One day, afar off in the desert, he descried a glittering

cavalcade—glittering it was indeed, for the horsemen were clad in armour of brass and steel, and the hot sun reflected the array like the march of a river of light. Arasmanes paused, and his heart swelled high within him as he heard through the wide plains the martial notes of the trumpet and the gong, and recognised the glory and pomp of war.

The cavalcade swept on; and the chief who rode at the head of the band paused as he surveyed with admiration the noble limbs, and proud stature, and dauntless eye of the Chaldæan. The chief summoned his interpreters; and in that age the languages of the east were but slightly dissimilar; so that the chief of the warriors conversed easily with the adventurer. "Know," said he, "that we are bent upon the most glorious enterprise ever conceived by the sons of men. In the farthest east there is a land of which thy fathers may have informed thee—a land of perpetual happiness and youth, and its name is Aden." Arasmanes started; he could scarce believe his ears. The warrior continued—"We are of that tribe which lies to the extremities of the east, and this land is therefore a heritage which we, of all the earth, have the right to claim. Several of our youth have at various times attempted to visit it, but supernatural agents have repelled the attempt. Now, therefore, that I have succeeded to the throne of my sires, I have resolved to invade and to conquer it by force of arms. Survey my band. Sawest thou ever, O Chaldæan, men of such limbs and stature, of such weapons of offence, and shields of proof? Canst thou conceive men more worthy of such a triumph, or more certain to attain it? Thou, too, art of proportions beyond the ordinary strength of men—thou art deserving to be one of us. Come, say the word, and the armourers shall clothe thee in steel, and thou shalt ride at my right hand."

The neighing of the steeds, and the clangour of the music, and the proud voice of the chieftain, all inspired the blood of Arasmanes. He thought not of the impiety of the attempt—he thought only of the glory: the object of his whole life seemed placed within his reach. He grasped at the offer of the warrior; and the armourer clad him in steel, and the ostrich plume waved over his brow, and he rode at the right hand of the warrior-king.

The armament was not without a guide; for, living so near unto the rising of the sun, what with others was tradition, with them was knowledge; and many amongst them had travelled to the site of Aden, and looked upon the black cloud that veiled it, and trembled at the sound of the rushing but invisible wings that hovered over.

Arasmanes confided to the warrior his whole history; they swore eternal friendship; and the army looked upon the Chaldæan as a man whom God had sent to their assistance. For, what was most strange, not one of the army ever seemed to imagine there was aught unholy or profane in the daring enterprise in which they had enlisted: accustomed to consider bloodshed a virtue, where was the crime of winning the gardens of Paradise by force?

Through wastes and deserts they held their way: and, though their numbers thinned daily by fatigue, and the lack of food, and the fiery breath of the burning winds, they seemed not to relax in their ardour, nor to repine at the calamities they endured.

Darkness gloomed like a wall! From heaven to earth stretched the palpable and solid Night that was the barrier to the land of Aden. No object gleamed through the impenetrable blackness; from those summitless walls hung no banner; no human champion frowned before the drear approach: all would have been silence, save that, at times, they heard the solemn rush as of some mighty sea; and they knew that it was the rush of the guardian wings.

The army halted before the Darkness, mute and awed; their eyes recoiled from the gloom, and rested upon the towering crest and snowy plumage of their chief. And he bade them light the torches of naphtha that they had brought with them, and unsheath their swords; and, at the given sound, horseman and horse dashed in through the walls of Night. For one instant, the torches gleamed and sparkled amidst the darkness, and were then suddenly extinguished; but through the gloom came one gigantic Hand wielding a sword of flame; and, wherever it turned, man smote the nearest man—father perished by his son—and brother fell gasping by the death-stroke of his brother; shrieks and cries, and the trample of affrighted steeds, rang through the riven shade—riven only by that mighty sword as it waved from rank to rank, and the gloom receded from its rays.

At eve the work was done; a small remnant of the warriors, alone escaped from the general slaughter, lay exhausted upon the ground before the veil of Aden. Arasmanes was the last who lingered in the warring gloom; for, as he lay struggling beneath the press of dying and the dead, the darkness had seemed to roll away, and, far into its depths, he caught one glimpse of the wonderful loveliness of Aden. There, over valleys covered with the greenest verdure, and watered by rivers without a wave, basked a purpling and loving sunlight that was peaceful and cloudless, for it was the smile of God. And there were groups of happy beings scattered around, in whose faces was the serenity of unutterable joy; even at the mere aspect of their happiness—happiness itself was reflected upon the soul of the Chaldæan, despite the dread, the horror, and the desolation of the hour. He stretched out his arms imploringly, and the vision faded for ever from his sight.

The king and all the principal chiefs of the army were no more; and with one consent, Arasmanes was proclaimed their leader. Sorrowful and dejected, he conducted the humbled remnant of the troop back through the deserts to the land they had so rashly left. Thrice on their return they were attacked by hostile tribes, but by the valour and prudence of Arasmanes they escaped the peril. They arrived at their native city to find that the brother of their chief had seized the reins of government. The army, who hated him, declared for the stranger-chief who had led them home. And Arasmanes, hurried away by the prospect of power, consented to their will. A battle ensued; the usurper was slain; and Arasmanes, a new usurper, ascended the throne in his stead.

The Chaldean was no longer young; the hardships he had undergone in the desert had combined with the anxieties that had preyed upon him during his residence in the City of Golden Palaces to plant upon his brow, and in his heart, the furrows of untimely age. He was in the possession of all the sources of enjoyment at that period when we can no longer enjoy. Howbeit, he endeavoured to amuse himself by his divan of justice, from which every body went away dissatisfied, and his banquets, at which the courtiers complained of his want of magnificence, and the people of his profligate expense. Grown wise by experience, he maintained his crown by flattering his army; and, surrounded by luxury, felt himself supported by power.

There came to the court of Arasmanes a strange traveller; he was a little old man, of plain appearance but great wisdom; in fact, he was one of the most noted sages of the East. His conversation though melancholy, had the greatest attraction for Arasmanes, who loved to complain to him of the cares of royalty, and the tediousness of his life.

"Ah, how much happier are those in an humble station!" said the king; "how much happier was I in the desert-cave, tending my herds, and listening to the sweet voice of Azraaph?—Would that I could recall those days!"

"I can enable you to do so, great king!" said the sage; "behold this mirror; gaze on it whenever you desire to recall the past; and whatever portion of the past you wish to summon to your eyes shall appear before you."

The sage did not deceive Arasmanes. The mirror reflected all the scenes through which the Chaldæan had passed: now he was at the feet of Chospor, a happy boy—now with elastic hopes entering into the enchanted valley of the Nymph ere yet he learned how her youth could fade—now he was at the source of little stream, and gazing on the face of Azraaph by the light of the earliest star; whichever of these scenes he wished to live over again reflected itself vividly in the magic mirror. Surrounded by pomp and luxury in the present, his only solace was in the past.

"You see that I was right," said he to the sage: "I was much happier in those days; else why so anxious to renew them?"

"Because, O great king!" said the sage, with a bitter smile, "you see them without recalling the feelings you then experienced as well as the scenes; you gaze on the past with the feelings you now possess, and all that then made the prospect clouded, is softened away by time. Judge for yourself if I speak true." So saying, the sage breathed over the mirror, and bade Arasmanes look into it once more. He did so. He beheld the same scenes, but the illusion was gone from them. He was a boy once more; but restlessness, and anxiety, and a thousand petty cares at his heart: he was again in the cave with Azraaph, but secretly pining at the wearisome monotony of his life: in all those scenes he now imagined the happiest, he perceived that he had not enjoyed the present; he had been looking forward to the future, and the dream of the unattainable Aden was at his heart. "Alas!" said he, dashing the mirror into pieces, "I was deceived; and thou hast destroyed for me, O sage, even the pleasure of the past!"

Arasmanes never forgot the brief glimpse of Aden that he had obtained in his impious warfare; and, now that the charm was gone from Memory, the wish yet to reach the unconquered land returned more powerfully than ever to his mind. He consulted the sage as to its possibility.

"Thou canst make but one more attempt" answered the wise man; and in that I cannot assist thee: but one who, when I am gone hence, will visit thee, shall lend thee her aid."

"Cannot the visitor come till thou art gone?" said Arasmanes.

"No, nor until my death," answered the sage.

This reply threw the mind of Arasmanes into great confusion. It was true he nowhere found so much pleasure as in the company of his friend—it was his only solace; but then, if he could never visit Aden (the object of his whole life) until that friend were dead!—the thought was full of affliction to him. He began to look upon the sage as an enemy, as an obstacle between himself and the possession of his wishes. He inquired every morning into the health of the sage; he seemed most provokingly strong. At length, from wishes for his death, dark thoughts came upon the Chaldæan; and he resolved to expedite it. One night the sage was found dead in his bed; he had been strangled by order of the king.

The very next day, as the king sat in his divan, a great noise was heard without the doors; and, presently, a hag, dressed in white garments of a foreign fashion, and of a hideous and revolting countenance, broke away from the crowd and made up to the king: "They would not let me come to thee, because I am homely and aged," said she in a shrill and discordant voice; "but I have been in a king's court before now—"

"What wantest thou woman?" said Arasmanes; and he felt, as he spoke, a chill creep to his heart.

"I am that visitor of which the wise man spoke," said she; "and I would talk to thee alone."

Arasmanes felt impelled as by some mighty power which he could not withstand; he rose from his throne, the assembly broke up in surprise, and the hag was admitted alone to the royal presence.

"Thou wouldst re-seek Aden, the land of Happiness and Truth?" said she, with a ghastly smile.

"Ay," said the king, and his knees knocked together.

"I will take thee thither."

"And when?"

"To-morrow, if thou wilt!" and the hag laughed aloud.

There was something in the manner, the voice, and the appearance of this creature so disgusting to Arasmanes, that he could brook it no longer. Aden itself seemed not desirable with such a companion and guide.

Without vouchsafing a reply he hastened from the apartment, and commanded his guards to admit the hag no more to the royal presence.

The sleep of Arasmanes that night was unusually profound, nor did he awaken on the following day till late at noon. From that hour he felt as if some strange revolution had taken place in his thoughts. He was no longer desirous of seeking Aden: whether or not the apparition of the hag had given him a distaste of Aden itself, certain it was that he felt the desire of his whole life had vanished entirely from his breast; and his only wish now was to enjoy, as long and as heartily as he was able, the pleasures that were within his reach.

"What a fool have I been," said he aloud, "to waste so many years in wishing to leave the earth! Is it only in my old age that I begin to find how much that is agreeable earth can possess?"

"Come, come, come!" cried a shrill voice; and Arasmanes, started, turned round to behold the terrible face of the hag.

"Come!" said she, stamping her foot; "I am ready to conduct thee to Aden."

"Wretch!" said the king, with quivering lips, "how didst thou baffle my guards? But I will strangle every one of them."

"Thou hast had enough of strangling," answered the crone, with a malignant glare. "Hast thou not strangled thy dearest friend?"

"What! tauntest thou me?" cried the king; and he rushed at the hag with his lifted sabre: the blade cut the air: the hag had shunned the blow; and, at the same moment, coming behind the king, she clasped him round the body, and fixed her long talons in his breast; through the purple robe, through the jewelled vest, pierced those vulture-fangs, and Arasmanes shrieked with terror and pain. The guards rushed in at the sound of his cry.

"Villains!" said he, as the cold drops broke from his brow, " would you leave me here to be murdered? Hew down yon hell hag; her death can only preserve life to you!"

"We saw her enter not, O King!" said the chief of the guards amazed; "but she shall now die the death." The soldiers, with one accord, made at the crone, who stood glaring at them like a hunted tigress.

"Fools!" said she, "know that I laugh alike at stone walls and armed men."

They heard the voice—they saw not whence it came—the hag had vanished.

The wound which the talons of this horrible visitor had made in the breast of the king refused to heal: it gave him excruciating anguish. The physicians tended him in vain; in vain, too, did the wise men preach patience and hope to him. What incensed him even more than the pain was the insult he had suffered—that such a loathsome and obscene wretch should dare to maim the person of a king!—the thought was not to be borne. But the more pain the king suffered, the more did he endeavour to court pleasure: life never seemed so charming to him as at the moment when it became an agony. His favourite courtiers, who had been accustomed to flatter his former weakness, and to converse with him about the happiness of Aden, and the possibility of entering it, found that even to broach the subject threw their royal master into a paroxysm of rage. He foamed at the mouth at the name of Aden—he wished, nay, he endeavoured to believe, that there was no such place in the universe.

At length one physician more sanguine than the rest, assured the king that he was able to cure the wound and relieve the pain.

"Know, O king!" said he, "that in the stream of Athron, which runneth through the valley of Mythra, there is a mystic virtue which can cure all the diseases of kings. Thou hast only to enter thy gilded bark, and glide down the stream for the space of twenty roods, scattering thine offering of myrrh and frankincense on the waters, in order to be well once more. Let the king live for ever!"

It was a dark, deep, and almost waveless stream; and the courtiers and the women, and the guards, and the wise men, gathered round the banks; and the king, leaning on the physician, ascended his gilded bark; and the physician alone entered the vessel with him. "For," said he, "the god of the stream loves it not to be profaned by the vulgar crowd; it is for kings only that it possesses its healing virtue."

So the king reclined in the middle of the vessel, and the physician took the censer of the precious odours; and the bark drifted down the stream, as the crowd wept and prayed upon the shore.

"Either my eyes deceive me," said the king, faintly, "or the stream seems to expand supernaturally, as into a great sea, and the shores on either side fade into distance."

"It is so," answered the physician. "And seest thou yon arch of black rocks flung over the tide?"

"Ay," answered the king.

"It is the approach to the land thou hast so often desired to reach: it is the entrance into Aden."

"Dog!" cried the king, passionately, "name not to me that hateful word."

As he spoke, the figure of the false physician shrunk in size, his robes fell from him,—and the king beheld in his stead the dwarfish shape of the accursed hag.

On drifted the vessel; and the crowd on the banks now beheld the hag seize the king in a close embrace: his shriek was wafted over the water, while the gorgeous vessel with its silken streamers and gilded sides, sped rapidly through the black arch of rocks: as the bark vanished, the chasm of the arch closed in, and the rocks uniting, presented a solid barrier to their gaze. But they shudderingly heard the ghastly laugh of the hag, piercing through the barrier, as she uttered the one word—"NEVER!" And from that hour the king was seen no more.

And this is the true history of Arasmanes, the Chaldæan.

CHAIROLAS

Once upon a time there existed a kingdom called Paida, stretching to the west of that wide tract of land known to certain ancient travellers by the name of Callipaga. The heirs apparent to the throne of this kingdom were submitted to a very singular ordeal. At the extremity of the empire was a chain of mountains, which separated Paida from an immense region, the chart of which no geographer had ever drawn. Various and contradictory were all the accounts of this region, from the oldest to the latest time. According to some it was the haunt of robbers and demons; every valley was beset with danger; the fruits of every tree were poisonous: and evil spirits lurked in every path, sometimes to fascinate, and sometimes to terrify, the inexperienced traveller to his destruction. Others, on the contrary, asserted that no land on earth equalled the beauty and the treasures of this mystic region. The purest air circulated over the divinest landscapes; the inhabitants were beneficient genii; and the life they led was that of happiness without alloy, and excitement without satiety. At the age of twenty the heir to the throne was ordained, by immemorial custom, to penetrate alone into this debated and enigmatical realm. It was supposed to require three years to traverse the whole of it, nor was it until this grand tour for the royalty of Paida was completed, that the adventurer was permitted to return home and aspire to the heritage of the crown. It happened, however, that a considerable proportion of these travellers never again re-entered their native land—detained, according to some, by the beautiful fairies of the unknown region; or, according to others, sacrificed by its fiends. One might imagine that those princes who were fortunate enough to return, too respectable travellers to be addicted to gratuitous invention, would have been enabled by their testimony to reconcile the various reports of the country into which they penetrated. But after their return the austere habits of royalty compelled them to discretion and reserve; and the hints which had escaped them from time to time, when conversing with their more confidential courtiers, so far from elucidating, confirmed the mystery; for each of the princes had evidently met with a different fortune: with one the reminiscences bequeathed by his journey seemed brilliant and delightful; while, perhaps, with his successor, the unknown region was never alluded to without a shudder or a sigh. Thus the only persons who could have reconciled conflicting rumours were exactly those who the most kept alive the debate; and the empire was still divided into two parties, who, according to the bias of their several dispositions, represented the neighbouring territory as an Elysium or a Tartarus.

The present monarch had of course undergone the customary ordeal. Naturally bold and cheerful, he had commenced his eventful journey with eagerness and hope, and had returned to Paida an altered and melancholy man. He swayed his people with great ability and success, he entered into all the occupations of his rank, and did not reject its pleasures and its pomps; but it was evident that his heart was not with his pursuits. He was a prey to some secret regret; but, whether he sighed to retain the land he had left, or was saddened by the adventures he had known, was a matter of doubt and curiosity even to his queen. Several years of his wedded life were passed without promise of an heir, and the eyes of the people were already turned to the eldest nephew of the sovereign, when it was formally announced to the court that the queen had been graciously pleased to become in the family-way.

In due process of time a son made his appearance. He was declared a prodigy of beauty, and there was something remarkably regal in the impatience of his cries. Nothing could exceed the joy of the court, unless it was the grief of the king's eldest nephew. The king himself, indeed, was perhaps also an exception to the general rapture; he looked wistfully on the crimson cheeks of his first-born, and muttered to himself, "These boys are a great subject of anxiety."

"And of pride," said a small sweet voice that came from the cradle.

The king was startled—for even in Paida a king's son does not speak as soon as he is born: he looked again at the little prince's face—it was not from him that the voice came, his royal highness had just fallen asleep.

"Dost thou not behold me, O king?" said the voice again.

And now the monarch beheld upon the pillow a small creature scarcely taller than a needle, but whose shape was modelled in the most beautiful proportions of manhood.

"Know," continued the apparition, while the king remained silent with consternation, "that I am the good genius of the new-born; each mortal hath at its birth his guardian spirit, though the genius be rarely visible. I bring to thy son the three richest gifts that can be bestowed upon man; but alas! they are difficult to preserve—teach him to guard them as his most precious treasure."

The genius vanished. The king recovered from his amaze, and, expecting to find some jewels of enormous value, hastily removed the coverlid, and saw by the side of his child an eagle's feather, a pigeon's feather, and a little tuft of the down of a swan.

The prince grew up strong, handsome, and graceful; he evinced the most amiable disposition; he had much of that tender and romantic enthusiasm which we call Sentiment, and which serves to render the virtues so lovely; he had an intuitive admiration for all that is daring and noble; and his ambition would, perhaps, have led him into dangerous excesses were it not curbed, or purified, by a singular disinterestedness and benevolence of disposition, which rendered him fearful to injure those with whom he came into contact, and anxious to serve them. The union of such qualities was calculated to conduct him to glory, but to render him scrupulous as to its means; his desire to elevate himself was strong, but it was blended with a stronger wish to promote the welfare of others. Princes of this nature were not common at Paida, and the people looked with the most sanguine hopes to the prospect of his reign. He had, however, some little drawbacks to the effect of his good qualities. His susceptibilities made him too easy with his friends, and somewhat too bashful with strangers; with the one he found it difficult to refuse any thing, with the other he was too keenly alive to ridicule and the fear of shame. But the first was a failing very easily forgiven at a court, and the second was one that a court would, in all probability, correct. The king took considerable pains with the prince's education, his talents were great, and he easily mastered whatever he undertook; but at each proof of the sweetness of his disposition, or the keenness of his abilities, the good king seemed to feel rather alarm than gratification. "Alas!" he would mutter to himself, "that fatal region—that perilous ordeal!" and then turn hastily away.

These words fed the prince's curiosity without much exciting his fear. The journey presented nothing terrible to his mind, for the courtiers, according to their wont, deemed it disloyal to detail to him any but the most flattering accounts of the land he was to visit; and he attributed the broken expressions of his father partly to the melancholy of his constitution, and partly to the over-acuteness of paternal anxiety. For the rest, it was a pleasant thing to get rid of his tutors and the formalities of a court; and with him, as with all the young, hope was an element in which fear could not breathe. He longed for his twentieth year, and forgot to enjoy the pleasures of boyhood in his anticipation of the excitements of youth.

The fatal time arrived; the Prince Chairolas had taken leave of his weeping mother—embraced his friends—and was receiving the last injunctions of his father, while his horses impatiently snorted at the gates of the palace.

"My son," said the king, with more than his usual gravity, "from the journey you are about to make you are nearly sure of returning a wiser man, but you may not return a better one. The three charms which you have always worn about your person you must be careful to preserve." Here the king recited, for the first time, to the wondering prince the adventure at his birth. Chairolas had always felt a lively curiosity to know why, from his infancy, he had been compelled to wear about his royal person three things, so apparently worthless, as an eagle's feather, a pigeon's feather, and the tuft of a swan's down, and still more why such seeming trifles had been gorgeously set in jewels. The secret now made known to him elevated his self-esteem; he was evidently, then, a favourite with the superior powers, and marked from his birth for no ordinary destinies.

"Alas!" concluded the king, "had I received such talismans, perhaps —" he broke off abruptly, once more embraced his son, and hastened to shroud his meditations in the interior of his palace.

Meanwhile the prince set out upon his journey: the sound of the wind instruments upon which the guards played cheerily, the caracoles of his favourite charger, the excitement of the fresh air, the sense of liberty, and the hope of adventure—all conspired to elevate his spirits. He forgot father, mother, and home. Never was journey undertaken under gayer presentiments, or by a more joyous mind.

At length the prince arrived at the spot where his attendants were to quit him. It was the entrance of a narrow defile through precipitous and lofty mountains. Wild trees of luxuriant foliage grew thickly along the path. It seemed a primeval vale, desolate even in its beauty, as though man had never trodden it before. The prince paused for a moment, his friends and followers gathered round him with their adieus, and tears, and wishes, but still Hope inspired and animated him; he waved his hand gaily, spurred his steed, and the trees soon concealed his form from the gaze of his retinue.

He proceeded for some time with slowness and difficulty, so entangled was the soil by its matted herbage, so obstructed was the path by the interlaced and sweeping boughs. At length, towards evening, the ground became more open; and, descending a gentle hill, a green and lovely plain spread itself before him. It was intersected by rivulets, and variegated with every species of plant and tree; it was a garden in which Nature seemed to have shewn how well she can dispense with Art. The prince would have been very much enchanted if he had not begun to be very hungry; and, for the first time, he recollected that it was possible to be starved. He looked anxiously, but vainly, round for some sign of habitation, and then he regarded the trees to see if they bore fruit; but, alas! it was the spring of the year, and he could only console himself with observing that the abundance of the blossoms promised plenty of fruit for the autumn,—a long time for a prince to wait for his dinner!

He still, however, continued to proceed, when suddenly he came upon a beaten track, evidently made by art. His horse neighed as its hoofs rang upon the hardened soil, and breaking of itself into a qucker pace, soon came to a wide arcade overhung with roses. "This must conduct to some mansion," thought Chairolas.

But night came on, and still the prince was in the arcade; the stars, peeping through, here and there, served to guide his course, until at length lights, more earthly and more brilliant, broke upon him. The arcade ceased, and Chairolas found himself at the gates of a mighty city, over whose terraces, rising one above the other, the moon shone bright and still.

"Who is there?" asked a voice at the gate.

"Chairolas, prince of Paida!" answered the traveller.

The gates opened instantly. "Princes are ever welcome at the city of Chrysaor," said the same voice.

And as Chairolas entered, he saw himself instantly surrounded by a group of both sexes richly attired, and bending to the earth with eastern adoration, while, as with a single voice, they shouted out, "Welcome to the Prince of Paida!"

A few minutes more, and Chairolas was in the magnificent

chamber of a magnificent house; the rarest viands, the richest wines, covered the board before him: and the attendants, with the most delicate sensibility, left him to himself.

"All this is delightful," thought the prince, as he finished his supper; "but I see nothing of either fairies or fiends."

His soliloquy was interrupted by the master of the mansion, who came to conduct the prince to his couch. Scarce was his head upon his pillow ere he fell asleep,—a sure sign that he was a stranger to Chrysaor, where the prevalent disease was the want of rest.

The next day, almost ere Chairolas was dressed, his lodging was besieged by all the courtiers of the city. He found that though his dialect was a little different from theirs, the language itself was much the same; for, perhaps, there is no court in the universe where a prince is not tolerably understood. The servile adulation which Chairolas had experienced in Paida was not nearly so delightful as the polished admiration he received from the courtiers of Chrysaor. While they preserved that tone of equality without which all society is but the interchange of ceremonies, they evinced, by a thousand nameless attentions, their respect for his good qualities, which they seemed to penetrate as by an instinct. The gaiety, the life, the grace of those he saw, perfectly intoxicated the prince. He was immediately involved in a round of engagements. It was impossible that he should ever be alone.

As the confusion of first impressions wore off, Chairolas remarked a singular peculiarity in the manners of his new friends. They were the greatest laughers he had ever met. Not that they laughed loud, or made much noise, but that they laughed constantly. This habit was not attended with any real merriment or happiness. Many of the saddest persons laughed the most. It was also remarkable that the principal objects of these cachinatory ebullitions were precisely such as Chairolas had been taught to consider the most serious, and the farthest removed from ludicrous associations. They never laughed at any thing witty or humorous, at a comedy or a joke. But if one of their friends became poor, then how they laughed at his poverty! If a child broke the heart of a father, or a wife ran away from her husband, or a great lord cheated at play, or ruined his tradesmen, then they had no command over their muscles. In a word, misfortune or vice made a principal object of the epidemical affection. But, besides this, they laughed at any thing that differed from their general habits. If a lady blushed—if a sage talked wisdom—if a man did anything uncommon, no matter what, they were instantly seized with jovial convulsion. They laughed at generosity—they laughed at sentiment—they laughed at patriotism—and, though affecting to be exceedingly pious, they laughed with particular pleasure at any extraordinary show of religion.

Chairolas was extremely puzzled; for he saw that if they laughed at what was bad, they laughed also at what was good: it seemed as if they had no other mode of condeming or applauding. But what perplexed him yet more was a strange transformation to which this people were subject. Their faces were apt to turn, even in a single night, into enormous rhododendrons; and it was very common to see a human figure walking about as gaily as possible with a flower upon its shoulders instead of a face.

Resolved to enlighten himself as to this peculiarity of custom, Chairolas one day took aside a courtier who appeared to him the most intelligent of his friends. Grinaldibus Hassan Sneeraskin (so was the courtier termed) laughed longer than ever when he heard the perplexity of the prince.

"Know," said he, as soon as he had composed himself, "that there are two penal codes in this city. For one set of persons, who you and I never see except in the streets,—persons who cut the wood and draw the water—persons who work for the other class,—we have punishments, such as hanging, and flogging, and shutting up in prisons, and Heaven knows what;—punishments, in short, that are contained in the ninety-nine volumes of the Hatchet and Rope Pandects. But for the other class, with whom you mix every day,—the very best society, in short,—we have another code, which punishes only by laughter. And you have no notion how severe the punishment is considered. It is thus that we keep our social system in order, and laugh folly and error out of countenance."

"An admirable—a most gentle code!" cried the prince. "But," he added, after a moment's reflection, "I see you sometimes laughing at what seems to me most praiseworthy, as well as most vicious."

"Not at all; your highness is mistaken: we never laugh at people who do exactly like the rest of us. We only laugh at whatever is odd; and with us oddity is a crime."

"Oddity even in virtue?"

"Precisely so."

"But those persons with rhododendrons instead of faces?"

"Are the worst of our criminals. If we continue to laugh at persons above a certain time, their faces undergo the transformation you have witnessed, no matter how handsome they were before."

"This is indeed laughing people out of countenance," said Chairolas, amazed. "What an affliction!"

"Indeed it is. Take care," added Grinaldibus Hassan Sneeraskin, with paternal unction,—"take care that you never do anything to deserve a laugh—the torture is inexpressible—the transformation is awful!"

This conversation threw Chairolas into a profound revery. The charm of the society was invaded; it now admitted restraint and fear. If ever he should be laughed at? If ever he should become a rhododendron?—terrible thought! He remembered various instances he had hitherto but little observed, in which he more than suspected that he had already been unconsciously afflicted with symptoms of this greatest of all calamities. His reason allowed the justice of his apprehension; for he could not flatter himself that in all respects he was exactly like the courtiers of Chrysaor.

That night he went to a splendid entertainment given by the prime minister. Conscious of great personal attractions, and magnificently attired, he felt, at his first entrance into the gorgeous hall, the flush of youthful and elated vanity. It was his custom to wear upon his breast one of his most splendid ornaments. It was the tuft of the fairy swan's down set in brilliants of great price. Something there was in this ornament which shed a kind of charm over his whole person. It gave a more interesting dignity to his mien, a loftier aspect to his brow, a deeper and a softer expression to his eyes. So potent is the present of a fairy, as all our science upon such subjects assures us.

Still, as Chairolas passed through the rooms, he perceived, with a thrill of terror, that a smile ill suppressed met him at every side; and when he turned his head to look back, he perceived that the fatal smile had broadened into a laugh. All his complacency vanished; terror and shame possessed him. Yes, he was certainly laughed at!

He felt his face itching already—certainly the leaves were sprouting!

He hastened to escape from the crowded rooms—passed into the lighted and voluptuous gardens—and seated himself in a retired and sequestered alcove. Here he was surprised by the beautiful Mikra, a lady to whom he had been paying assiduous court, and who appeared to take a lively interest in his affairs.

"Prince Chairolas here!" cried the lady, seating herself by his side; "alone too, and sad! How is this?"

"Alas!" answered the prince, despondingly, "I feel that I am regarded as a criminal: how can I hope for your love! In a word— dreadful confession!—I am certainly laughed at. I shall assuredly blossom in a week or two. Light of my eyes! deign to compassionate about my affliction, and inform my ignorance. Acquaint me with the crime I have committed."

"Prince," said the gentle Mikra, much moved by her lover's dejection, "do not speak thus. Perhaps I ought to have spared you this pain. But then delicacy restrained me—"

"Speak—speak in mercy!"

"Well then—but pardon me—that swan's down tuft, it is charming, beautiful, it becomes you exceedingly! But at Chrysaor nobody wears swan's down tufts,—you understand."

"And it is for this, then, that I may be rhododendronized!" exclaimed Chairolas.

"Indeed, I fear so."

"Away treacherous gift!" exclaimed the prince; and he tore off the fairy ornament. He dashed it to the ground, and left the alcove. The fair Mikra stayed behind to pick up the diamonds: the swan's down itself had vanished, or, at least, it was invisible to the fine lady of Chrysaor.

With the loss of his swan's down Prince Chairolas recovered his self-complacency. No one laughed at him in future. He was relieved from the fear of efflorescence. For a while he was happy. But months glided away, and the prince grew tired of his sojourn at Chrysaor. The sight of the same eternal faces and the same eternal rhododendrons, the sound of the same eternal laughter, wearied him to death. He resolved to pursue his travels. Accordingly, he quarrelled with Mikra, took leave of his friends, and, mounting his favourite steed, departed from the walls of Chyrsaor. He took the precaution, this time, of hiring some attendants at Chrysaor, who carried with them provisions. A single one of the many jewels he bore about him would have more than sufficed to purchase the service of half Chrysaor.

Although he had derived so little advantage from one of the fairy gifts, he naturally thought he might be more fortunate with the rest. The pigeon's feather was appropriate enough to travelling (for we may suppose that it was a carrier pigeon); accordingly he placed it, set in emeralds, amidst the plumage of his cap. He spent some few days in rambling about, until he found he had entered a country unknown even to his guides. The landscape was more flat and less luxuriant than that which had hitherto cheered his way, the sun was less brilliant, and sky seemed nearer to the earth.

While gazing around him, he became suddenly aware of the presence of a stranger, who, stationed right before his horse, stretched forth his hand and thus accosted him:—

"O thrice-noble and generous traveller! save me from starvation. Heaven smiles upon one to whom it has given the inestimable treasure of a pigeon's feather. May Heaven continue to lavish its blessings upon you,—meanwhile spare me a trifle!"

The charitable Chairolas ordered his purse-bearer to relieve the wants of the stranger, and then inquired the name of the country they had entered. He was informed that it was termed Apatia; and that its inhabitants were singularly cordial to travellers, "Especially," added the mendicant, "if they possess that rarest of earthly gifts—the feather of a pigeon."

"Well," thought Chairolas, "my good genius evidently intends to make up for his mistake about the swan's down: doubtless the pigeon's feather will be exceedingly serviceable!"

He desired the mendicant to guide him to the nearest city of Apatia, which, fortunately, happened to be the metropolis.

On entering the streets, Chairolas was struck with the exceeding bustle and animation of the inhabitants; far from the indolent luxury of Chrysaor, every thing breathed of activity, enterprise, and toil.

The place resembled a fortfified town; the houses were built of ponderous stone, a drawbridge to each; the windows were barred with iron; a sentinel guarded every portico.

"Is there a foreign invasion without the walls?" asked the prince.

"No," answered the mendicant; "but here every man guards against his neighbour, take care of yourself, noble sir;" so saying, the grateful Apatian picked the prince's pockets, and disappeared amidst the crowd.

The prince found himself no less courted at the capital of Apatia then he had been in Chrysaor. But society was much less charming. He amused himself by going out in the streets incognito, and watching the manners of the inhabitants. He found them addicted to the most singular pursuits. One game consisted in setting up a straw and shooting arrows at it blindfold. If you missed the mark, you paid dearly; if you hit it, you made a fortune. Many persons ruined themselves at this game.

Another amusement consisted in giving certain persons, trained for the purpose, and dressed in long gowns, a quantity of gold, in return for which they threw dirt at you. The game was played thus:— You found one of these gownsmen—gave him the required quantity of gold—and then stood to be pelted at in a large tennis-court; your adversary did the same:— if the gownsman dirtied your antagonist, you were stripped naked and turned adrift in the streets; but if your antagonist was the most bespattered, you won your game, and received back half the gold you had given to your gownsman. This was a most popular diversion. They had various other amusements, all of the same kind, in which the chief entertainment was the certainty of loss.

For the rest, the common occupation was quarrelling with each other, buying and selling, picking pockets, and making long speeches about liberty and glory!

Chairolas found that the pigeon's feather was everywhere a passport to favour. But in a short time this produced its annoyances. His room was besieged by applications for charity. In vain he resisted. No man with a pigeon's feather, he was assured, ever refused assistance to the poor. All the ladies in the city were in love with him; plundered him; and the reason of the adoration and the plunder was the pigeon's feather.

One day he found his favourite friend with his favourite fair one—a fair one so favoured, that he had actually proposed and had actually been accepted. Their familiarity and their treachery were evident. Chairolas drew his sabre, and would certainly have slain them both, if the lady's screams had not brought the king's guards into the room. They took all three before the judge. He heard the case gravely, and sentenced Chairolas to forego the lady and pay the costs of the sentence.

"Base foreigner that you are!" he said, gravely, "and unmindful of your honour. Have you not trusted your friend and believed in her you loved? Have you not suffered them to be often together? If you had been an honourable man, you would know that you must always watch a woman and suspect a friend.—Go!"

As Chairolas was retiring, half-choked with rage and shame, the lady seized him by the arm. "Ah!" she whispered, "I should never have deceived you but for the pigeon's feather."

Chairolas threw himself on his bed, and, exhausted by grief, fell fast asleep. When he woke the next morning, he found that his attendants had disappeared with the bulk of his jewels: they left behind them a scroll containing these words—"A man with so fine a pigeon's feather will never hang us for stealing."

Chairolas flung the feather out of the window. The wind blew it away in an instant. An hour afterwards he had mounted his steed and was already beyond the walls of the capital of Apatia.

At nightfall the prince found himself at the gates of a lofty castle. Wearied and worn out, he blew the horn suspended at the portals, and demanded food and shelter for the night. No voice answered, but the gates opened of their own accord. Chairolas left his courser to feed at will on the herbage, and entered the castle: he passed through several magnificent chambers without meeting a soul till he came to a small pavilion. The walls were curiously covered with violets and rose-leaves wrought in mosaic; the lights streamed from jewels of a ruby glow, set in lotos-leaves. The whole spot breathed of enchantment; in fact, Chairolas had at length reached an enchanted castle.

Upon a couch in an alcove reclined a female form, covered with a veil studded with silver stars, but of a texture sufficiently transparent to permit Chairolas to perceive how singularly beautiful were the proportions beneath. The prince approached with a soft step.

"Pardon me," he said, with an hesitating voice, "I fear that I disturb your repose." The figure made no reply; and, after a pause, Chairolas, unable to resist the desire to see the face of the sleeper, lifted the veil.

Never had so beautiful a countenance broke even upon his dreams. The first bloom of youth shed its softest hues over the cheek; the lips just parted in a smile which sufficed to call forth a thousand dimples. Nothing was wanting to complete the most perfect ideal of virgin beauty, save the eyes; but these were closed in a slumber so profound, that but for the colours of the cheek and the regular and ambrosial breathing of the lips, you might have imagined that the slumber was of death. Beside her, on the couch, lay a casket, on which the eyes of the prince, resting, caught these works engraved—"He alone who can unlock this casket will waken the sleeper; and he who finds the heart may claim the hand."

Chairolas, transported with joy and hope, seized the casket—

118

the key was in the lock. With trembling hands he sought to turn it in the hasp—it remained immovable—it resisted his most stenuous efforts. Nothing could be more slight than the casket—more minute than the key; but all the strength of Chairolas was insufficient to open the lock.

Chairolas was in despair. He remained for days—for weeks in the enchanted chamber. He neither ate not slept during all that time. But such was the magic of the place that he never once felt hunger or fatigue. Gazing upon that divine form, he for the first time felt all the rapture and intoxication of real love. He spent his days and nights in seeking to unclose the casket; sometimes in his rage he dashed it to the ground—he trampled upon it—he sought to break what he could not open—in vain.

One day while thus employed, he heard the horn wind without the castle gates; then steps echoed along the halls, and presently a stranger entered the enchanted pavilion. The new-comer was neither old nor young, neither handsome nor ugly. He approached the alcove despite the menacing looks of the jealous prince. He gazed upon the sleeper; and, as he gazed, a low music breathed throughout the chamber. Surprised and awed, Chairolas let the casket fall from his hands. The intruder took it from the ground, read the inscription, and applied his hand to the key;—it turned not;—Chairolas laughed aloud;—the stranger sighed, and drew forth from his breast a little tuft of swan's down—he laid it upon the casket—again turned the key—the casket opened at once, and within lay a small golden heart. At that instant a voice broke from the heart. "Thou hast found the charm," it said; and, at the same time, the virgin woke, and as she bent her eyes upon the last comer, she said, with unutterable tenderness, "It is of thee, then, that I have so long dreamed." The stranger fell at her feet. And Chairolas, unable to witness his rival's happiness, fled from the pavilion.

"Accursed that I am!" he groaned aloud. "If I had not cast away the fairy gift, *she* would have been mine!"

For several days the unfortunate prince wandered through the woods and wastes, supporting himself on wild berries, and venting, in sighs and broken exclamations, his grief and rage. At length he came to the shores of a wide and glassy sea,—a sea more lovely than ever in the odorous south basking in the purpling hues of an Ausonian sun. Its waves crisped over golden sands with a delicious and heavenly music; the air was scented with

119

unspeakable fragrance, wafted from trees peculiar to the clime, and bearing at the same time the blossom and the fruit. At a slight distance from the shore was an island which seemed one garden—the fabled bowers of the Hesperides.[1] Studded it was with ivory palaces, delicious fountains, and streams that wound amidst groves of asphodel and amaranth. And everywhere throughout the island wandered groups whose faces the prince could distinctly see, and those faces were made beautiful by unruffled peace and happiness unalloyed. Laughter—how different from that of Chrysaor!—was wafted to his ear, and the boughs of the trees, as they waved to the fragrant wind, gave forth melodies more exquisite than ever woke from the lyres of Lycia or Ionia.[2]

Wearied and exhausted, the prince gazed upon the Happy Isle, and longed to be a partaker of its bliss, when, turning his eyes a little to the right, he saw, from a winding in the shore on which he stood, a vessel, with silken streamers, seemingly about to part for the opposite isle. Several persons of either sex were crowding into the vessel, and already waving their hands to the groups upon the island. Chairolas hastened to the spot. He pushed impatiently through the crowd; he was about to enter the vessel, when a venerable old man stopped and accosted him.

"Would you go, stranger, to the Happy Isle?"

"Yes! Quick—quick, let me pass!"

"Stranger, whoever would enter the vessel must comply first with the conditions and pay the passage."

"I have some jewels left still," said Chairolas, haughtily. "I will pay the amount ten times over."

"We require neither jewels nor money," returned the old man, gravely. "What you must produce is the feather of a pigeon."

Chairolas shrunk back aghast. "But," said he, "I have no longer a pigeon's feather!"

The old man gazed at him with horror. The passengers set up a loud cry—"He has no pigeon's feather!" They pushed him back, the vessel parted, and Chairolas was left upon the strand.

Cursing his visits to Chrysaor and Apatia, which had cost him so dear and given him so little in return, Chairolas tore himself from the sea-shore and renewed his travels.

Towards the noon of the following day he entered a valley covered with immense sunflowers and poppies. Anything so gaudy he had never before beheld. Here and there were rocks, evidently not made by nature;—mounds raised by collections of various rubbish, ornamented with artificial ruins and temples. Sometimes he passed through grottoes formed by bits of coloured glass and shells, intended to imitate spars and even jewels. The only birds that inhabited the boughs were parrots and mock-birds. They made a most discordant din; but they meant it for imitations of nightingales and canaries. The flare of the poppies and the noise of the birds were at first intolerable, but by degrees the wanderer became used to them, and at length found them charming.

"How delightful this is!" said he, flinging himself under a yew-tree, which was cut in the shape of a pagoda. "So cheerful—so gay! After all I am as well off here as in the Happy Isle. Nay, I think there is a greater air of comfort in the sight of these warm sunflowers than in those eternal amaranths; and certainly, the music of these parrots in exceedingly lively!"

While thus soliloquising the prince saw an old baboon walk leisurely up to him. The creature supported itself upon a gold-headed staff. It wore a long wig and a three-cornered hat. It had a large star of coloured glass on its breast; and an apron of sky-blue round its middle.

As the baboon approached, Chairolas was much struck by its countenance; the features were singularly intelligent and astute, and seemed even more so from a large pair of spectacles, which gave the animal a learned look about the eyes.

"Prince!" said the baboon, "I am well acquainted with your adventures, and I think I can be of service to you in your present circumstances."

"Can you give me the lady I saw in the enchanted castle?"

"No!" answered the baboon. "But a man who has seen so much of the world knows, that after a little time one lady is not better than another."

"Can you then admit me to the Happy Isle?"

"No! but you said rightly just now, that this valley was at least as agreeable."

"Can you give me back my tuft of swan's down and my pigeon's feather?"

"No! but I can imitate them so exactly that the imitations will be equally useful. Meanwhile, come and dine with me."

Chairolas followed the baboon into a cave, where he was

sumptuously served by pea-green monkeys to dishes of barbecued squirrels.

After dinner the baboon and the prince renewed their conversation. From his host, Chairolas learned that the regions called "the unknown" by the people of Paida, were of unlimited extent, inhabited by various nations; that no two of his predecessors had ever met with the same adventures, though most of them had visited both Chrysaor and Apatia. He was, indeed, an animal of exceeding age and experience, and had a perfect recollection of the cities before the deluge.

He made out of the silky hair of a white fox, a most excellent imitation of the tuft of swan's down: and from the breast of a vulture, he plucked a feather which any one at a distance might mistake for a pigeon's.

Chairolas received them with delight.

"And now, prince," said the baboon, "observe, that while you may show these as openly as you please, it will be prudent to conceal the eagle's feather that you have yet left. No inconvenience results from parading the false,—much danger from exhibiting the true. Take this little box of adamant, lock up the eagle's feather in it, and whenever you meditate any scheme or exploit, open it and consult the feather. In future you will find that it has a voice, and can answer when you speak to it."

Chairolas stayed some days in the baboon's valley, and then once more renewed his travels. What was his surprise to find himself, on the second day of his excursion, in the same defile as that which had conducted him from his paternal realms. He computed, for the first time, the months he had spent in his wanderings, and found that the three years were just accomplished. In less than an hour the prince was at the mouth of the defile, where a numerous cavalcade had been for some days assembled to welcome his return and conduct him home.

The young prince was welcomed at Paida with the greatest enthusiasm. Every one found him prodigiously improved. He appeared in public with the false swan's down and the false pigeon's feather. They became him even better than the true ones, and he indeed had taken care to have them set in much more magnificent jewels. But the prince was a prey to one violent and master passion—Ambition. This, indeed had always been a part of his character; but previous to his travels it had been guided by generous and patriotic impulses. It was so no longer. He spent whole days in conversing with the eagle's feather though the feather, indeed, never said but one word, which was—"WAR."

At that time a neighbouring people had chosen five persons instead of two to inspect the treasury accounts. Chairolas affected to be horror-struck with the innovation. He declared it boded no good to Paida; he declaimed against it night and day. At last, he so inflamed the people, that, despite the reluctance of the king, war was declared. An old general of great renown headed the army. Chairolas was appointed second in command. They had scarely reached the confines of the enemy's country, when Chairolas became no less unhappy than before. "Second in command! why not first?" He consulted his demon feather. It said, "FIRST." It spoke no other word. The old general was slow in his movements; he pretended that is was unwise to risk a battle at so great a distance from the capital; but in reality, he hoped the appearance of his army would awe the enemy into replacing the two treasurers, and so secure the object of the war without bloodshed. Chairlos penetrated this design, so contrary to his projects. He wrote home to his father, to accuse the general of taking bribes from the enemy. The old king readily believed one whom the fairy had so endowed. The general was recalled and beheaded. Chairolas succeeded to the command. He hastened to march to the city, which he took and burned; but, instead of replacing the two treasurers, he appointed one chief—himself; and twenty subordinate treasurers—his officers.

Never was prince so popular as Chairolas on his return from his victories. He was intoxicated by the sweetness of power and the desire of yet greater glory. He longed to reign himself—he sighed to think his father was so healthy. He shut himself up in his room and talked to his feather; its word now was "KING." Shortly afterwards Chairolas (who was the idol of the soldiers) seized the palace, issued a proclamation that his father was in his dotage, and had abdicated the throne in his favour. The king was put into prison, and a day or two afterwards found dead in his bed. Chairolas mourned for three months, and everybody compassionated his grief.

From that time Chairolas, now the monarch of Paida, gave himself up to his ruling passion. He extended his fame from east to west—he was called the Great Chairolas. But his subjects became tired or war; their lands were ravaged—their treasury exhausted— new taxes were raised for new conquests, and at length Chairolas was no longer called the "Great," but the "Tyrant."

As Chairolas advanced in years, he left off wearing the false swan's down and the false pigeon's feather. He had long ceased to lock up his eagle-plume; he carried it constantly in his helmet, that it might whisper with ease into his ear. He had ceased to be popular with any class the moment he abandoned the presents of the baboon. By degrees a report spread through the nation that the king was befriended by an evil spirit, and that the eagle's plume was a talisman which secured to the possessor—while it rendered him grasping, cruel, and avaricious—prosperity, power and fame. A conspiracy was formed to rob the king of his life and talisman at once. At the head of the conspiracy was the king's heir, Belmanes. They took their measures so well, that they succeeded in seizing the palace. They penetrated into the chamber of the Great Chairolas,—they paused at the threshold on hearing his voice,—he was addressing the fatal talisman.

"The ordeal," he said, "through which I passed robbed me of thy companions; but no ordeal could rob me of thee. I rule my people with a rod of iron; I have spread my conquests to the farthest regions to which the banner of Paida was ever wafted. I am still dissatisfied—what more can I desire?"

"Death!" cried the conspirators; and the king fell pierced to the heart. Belmanes seized the eagle's plume: it crumbled into dust in his grasp.

After the death of Chairolas, the following sentences were written in gold letters before the gates of the great academy of Paida by a priest who pretended to be inspired:—

"The ridicule of common men aspires to be the leveller of genius."

"To renounce a virtue, because it has made thee suffer from fraud, is to play the robber to thyself."

"Wouldst thou imitate the properties of the swan and the pigeon, borrow from the fox and the vulture. But no man can wear the imitations all his life: when he abandons them, he is undone."

"If thou hast three virtues, and losest two, the third, by itself, may become a vice. There is no blessing to the world like AMBITION, joined to SYMPATHY and BENEVOLENCE; no scourge to the world, like ambition divorced from them."

"The choicest gifts of the most benevolent genii are impotent,

124

unless accompanied by a charm against experience."

"The charm against experience is woven by two spirits—Patience and Self-esteem."

On these sentences nine sects of philosophy were founded. Each construed them differently; each produced ten thousand volumes in support of its interpretation; and no man was ever made better or wiser by the sentences, the sects, and the volumes.

THE THREE SISTERS

Translated from the Phoenician by
the author of "Eugene Aram", &c

In an age which two or three thousand years ago was
considered somewhat of the earliest, but which geologists have
proved to have been but as yesterday, Iao-pater reigned over those
districts known to historians by the name of Phoenicia. An honest,
arbitrary, good sort of King he was; not altogether unlike our
Henry the Eighth,—only he was not quite so much master of his
own house. Her majesty led him a troublesome life—into the
particulars of which we need not enter, seeing that people in this
virtuous age have a disinclination to scandal, and that the Greeks
have made some of the best stories sufficiently familiar in that
budget of gossip which they call a Mythology.

Revenons a nos moutons.[1]

Iao-pater had a very large family—sons and daughters without
number. Amongst them, by a left-handed marriage,[2] were three
young ladies, called, in the language of that day, Aza, Merthyne,
and Insla. Respecting these princesses, we find a tale recorded in
one of the manuscripts consulted by Sanchoniathon, in his work
on the Serpent, which has not hitherto been published.

In the latter days of Iao-pater his subjects were visited by a
most terrible species of madness. Each man fancied he saw a
horrible dragon upon the back of his neighbour, and was instantly
seized with a furious desire to attack the monster. Thus, the
moment your back was turned, half-a-dozen of your countrymen
made a rush at you, one with a sword, to hew, another with a saw,
to saw, a third with redhot pincers, to pluck off, the creature of
their imagination: if no other weapon was at hand, they fastened
on you with their nails and teeth. What made this malady more
singular, while their victim perished under their mutilations, they
kept congratulating him on his approaching delivery from the
dragon. The more he bellowed for mercy, the worse he fared: when
once attacked in this manner, his fate was sealed, and, as he gave
up the ghost, his tormentors, instead of suspecting they had done
anything wrong, shrugged their shoulders, and cried— "This
comes of the dragon! "

So dreadful were the ravages and slaughter resulting from this insanity, that his majesty's dominions were nearly depopulated. Iao-pater, in a great fright lest his own back should be caught sight of, shut himself up in his palace; and all prudent persons, following the royal example, kept themselves in-doors, with their backs screwed tight against the wall. The sooth-sayers killed nine millions and forty-two birds, and four hundred thousand sows, but the entrails of the victims were obstinately silent on the occasion, nor could any remedy for the growing evil be suggested by councillor or priest.

At length, one night, Aza dreamed a dream. She thought that the great deity, No-No, appeared to her, and said—"Arise, go forth into the city, and the people shall be delivered from the curse." And Aza, the next morning, sought Iao-pater, who had crept into a hole of the wall, so that nothing but his face was discernible. Aza told her dream, and implored permission to obey the divine command.

"Do as you like, my dear child," said the King; "but don't come so close to me: and mind, wherever you go, that you proclaim it to be high treason to attempt to peep at my back. As for other people's backs—it is not my affair."

When Aza went forth from the palace, she repaired to the royal gardens, and amused herself with catching the most beautiful butterflies she could find. Having put them into a little net of silver meshes, inconceivably fine, she took her way into the great street. Scarcely had she gone three paces, when she heard a tremendous uproar and hallooing; and presently a young man, more beautiful than words can describe, came bounding up the street, pale, breathless, and frightened out of his wits, and fell exhausted at the feet of the princess.

"Save me!—save me!" he cried out. "I am an unhappy stranger in this city, and a whole mob are at my heels, swearing I have a dragon on my back. As long as I spoke to them face to face they overwhelmed me with civilities. But the moment I turned!—Ah, here they are!" And, in fact, a score or two of fierce-looking citizens, some with hatchets, some with pincers, some with long hooks—{all for the dragon}—now thronged, hot and panting, on the spot.

At the sight of Aza they halted abruptly—for there was something in her face so serene and lovely, that even those wretched maniacs felt the soothing influence of her beauty.

"My friends," said Aza, in a voice of sweet command, "what would you with this young man?"

"The dragon! the dragon!—shouted a dozen voices, already hoarse with screaming—"He has a dragon on his back; we would not harm him for the world!—a most charming young man!—but the dragon, your royal highness,—the dragon!"

"I have taken if off the stranger's back," said the princess, mildly. "See, here it is. Behold the terrible monster that so appals you!" So saying, she opened her hand, and away flew one of the most beautiful purple and gold butterflies that ever was seen.

As the insect fluttered and circled to and fro, the crowd stared at it with open mouths.

"Bless me," cried one of them, "and that's what we took for a dragon,—so it is!'

"Hollo! you sir!" cried another, lifting up his hatchet against the last speaker, who had unwittingly turned round and exposed his own back—"The dragon is on you!"

"Hold!" exclaimed Aza, arresting the madman's arm. "The god No-No has changed all your dragons into butterflies." With that, she turned aside, and unperceived by the crowd, emptied the silver net. The air was filled with butterflies. The crowd stared again; first at the insects, then at the princess, then at one another. Fortunately, at that time the god No-No thought it a good opportunity to thunder: the omen completed the cure—and the mob woke all at once from their delusion.

Twenty men in their senses are sometimes enough to convert a multitude of maniacs; and those who were now convinced that dragons were butterflies, went about proclaiming the miraculous fact, till at last they persuaded or frightened the rest of the citizens into that belief. But scarce was this epidemic over, than a new disease seized this ill-fated people. They took it into their heads, that Iao-pater, in order to punish them for their recent inhumanity, had covered the streets with invisible man-traps; and the moment this crotchet seized them, not a mother's son would budge a foot! There—where the idea first entered a man—there he stood, as still as a stone. He would not even stir for food. Thousands were starved to death. Business was suspended. The whole city seemed attacked with the rot.

Poor Aza found all her exhortations and artifices useless; and was returning sorrowfully to the palace with the young stranger, who was lost in astonishment at the singular set into which he had fallen, when she met her youngest sister, Merthyne, who was then but a child.

"You are surprised to see me here," said the latter; "but the god No-No has just appeared to me. 'Merthyne,' said the god, 'arise, go into the city, and the people shall be delivered from the curse.'"

"I am surprised," said Aza, who, with all her amiable qualities, could not help being a little jealous that her sister was favoured equally with herself; "I am surprised that the god No-No should appear to such a child as you are. But no matter;—only some people don't always tell the truth."

This last aphorism contained a very just sarcasm; for Merthyne was by no means scrupulously veracious. But then she told fibs with so much grace and so little malice, and was altogether such a charming, smiling, pretty little creature, that she was the darling of the whole family. She made no reply to Aza's taunt; but, shaking her golden locks archly, went singing through the streets.

She soon came to a grave old judge, who was standing spellbound on one leg, not daring to put down the other, though he was ready to drop with fatigue.

"Bless your gray hairs," cried Merthyne gaily; "why, how young you look! I need not wish you long life—you'll live these fifty years!"

"You are very good, child," said the judge gruffly; "but how I am to live long with a great man-trap ready to catch me by the leg, is more than -"

"Man-trap! Stuff!" interrupted Merthyne; "come, I want you to play at hide-and-seek with me!"

So saying, the little princess picked up a straw that lay on the ground, began tickling the judge's foot as it hung rampant in the air, till at last he was forced, between scolding and laughing to put it down. No sooner had he done this , than little Merthyne drew a rattle from her bosom, and began skipping before him, and sounding the rattle so merrily in his ears, that the old judge could not for the life of him withstand it.

"You provoking little creature," he cried, "I must and will have a kiss from these laughing lips."

"Catch me, if you can," cried Merthyne, skipping and rattling with all her might.

The judge made a start. Away ran Merthyne; and the judge hobbled after her as fast as he could. He could not go fast, indeed;

for, besides that he was gouty, he had the pleasure to find that, in lifting his feet from the ground, he took away the great baked pieces of clay on which he had been standing, and which, in that city, answered the purpose of paving-stones. And there was this beautiful little fairy dancing, meteor-like, before him; and there was the gouty old judge dancing after her, with two huge pieces of pavement sticking to his feet! Away they went through the market-place; and so seductive was Merthyne's rattle, and so contagious was the judge's unwonted friskiness, that every body they passed forgot the man-traps and scampered after them; each, like the judge, taking up the piece of clay on which he stood. The noise of this extraordinary crowd, all dancing, and laughing, and clattering through the streets, was so great, that those who were in their houses ran to the window; but no sooner did they see the procession, and catch a glance of Merthyne's glad eyes, than they ran out, carrying the floor with them at the soles of their shoes.

In this manner Merthyne had gone through the whole city, and was now leading the dance round the palace, when old Iao-pater himself popped his head out of his door, and saw the new mania that seized upon his subjects.

"Did ever king rule over such a strange people!" cried he; "what is to be done now? Where are the priests and soothsayers?"

"Dancing away, your majesty, as mad as the rest of them," said the grave Insla, a young woman of a very serious cast of character.

"More shame for them," said the king; "yet I must own I feel the fidgets myself. What a dear little creature that Merthyne is! Zounds! my feet itch to have a dance! Tum-tum-tira-tira-tum!"

"My dear father," said Insla, "this morning I dreamed a dream. The god No-No appeared to me and said, 'Insla, it shall come to pass that thou shalt see men dancing with clods at their feet. When thou lookest at them, go forth; and the feet shall be released from the clay."

"That would be a great comfort," said the king; "it must be very fatiguing to be so heavily shod. Go, my child; the god No-No must never be disobeyed."

Having thus got the king's permission, Insla went into the back garden, where there was at a that time an old balloon (for we are not the new inventors we think for). It had not been used for a long time; and was thrown aside as a piece of old-fashioned lumber. She summoned the slaves to arrange and inflate the balloon; and, in the meanwhile, she went into the treasury, and selected several jewels of extraordinary lustre. These she fastened to gold threads, so fine as to be invisible at a little distance; and having mounted the balloon, she suspended the threads at the sides of the aerial vehicle. The slaves cut the string over the heads of the clamorous multitude. At the sight of the pendent jewels glittering in the sunlight, the crowd stood still; and even Merthyne suspended her rattle.

"Sons of men!" said Insla in a sonorous and majestic voice; "behold the proper objects of desire! Each of these jewels is more valuable than a Kingdom! See! they hang but little above your heads; you have but to leap high enough to grasp them!"

The crowd turned their bewildered eyes to Merthyne; for so had that mischievous little baggage fascinated them, that they would not have stirred a step without her instigation. But Merthyne was herself dazzled, childlike, by the jewels; and shaking her rattle, she tripped to the spot over which the balloon hovered, and began to jump as high as she could, in order to catch a superb emerald that seemed just within her reach. Her example was instantly followed; the judges and the soothsayers, the old and the young, all began to jump; and with such heartiness and energy, that one after the other, they kicked off the clods of clay that had stuck to their feet; and they seemed in a fair way catching the balloon and all its treasures, when Insla, seeing her object was effected, mounted gradually higher and higher, and vanished from the disappointed eyes of the crowd.

It was then that a sudden splendour broke over the whole city; and the soothsayers fell flat on the ground, crying out, "The god No-No!" A mighty and gigantic shadow, like that of some Colossus, grew into shape in the midst of the blaze of light; and a sweet low voice thus spoke:

"Well have ye performed your parts, daughters of Iao-pater; and immortal life have you obtained as your reward. For thee and thine other progeny, O king! is reserved the destiny of translation to the skies. Human as ye are, ye will be honoured as gods by many generations and in the fairest lands. But the empire of Aza, Merthyne, and Insla, will be more permanent and more durable. Go forth, ye Blessed Three, over the whole world; not borne aloft to Olympus, but destined to hold your sway below, wherever the heart beats and the mind aspires. Take with you the gift of eternal youth; and be known amongst mortals by names honoured in every tongue—CHARITY, HOPE and FAITH."

Thus ends the apologue in the original Phoenician. I have no doubt that the story is perfectly true, having, myself, often listened to the rattle of Merthyne, and gazed on the balloon of Insla:—as for Aza, or Charity, I confess I never had the pleasure of meeting her in polite society.

THE HAUNTED AND THE HAUNTERS;
or, The House and the Brain

A friend of mine, who is a man of letters and a philosopher, said to me one day, as if between jest and earnest: "Fancy! since we last met, I have discovered a haunted house in the midst of London."

"Really haunted?—and by what? — ghosts?"

"Well, I can't answer that question; all I know is this: six weeks ago my wife and I were in search of a furnished apartment. Passing a quiet street, we saw on the window of one of the houses a bill, 'Apartments, Furnished.' The situation suited us: we entered the house—liked the rooms—engaged them by the week—and left them the third day. No power on earth could have reconciled my wife to stay longer; and I don't wonder at it."

"What did you see?"

"Excuse me—I have no desire to be ridiculed as a superstitious dreamer, nor, on the other hand, could I ask you to accept on my affirmation what you would hold to be incredible without the evidence of your own senses. Let me only say this, it was not so much what we saw or heard (in which you might fairly suppose that we were the dupes of our own excited fancy, or the victims of imposture in others) that drove us away, as it was an undefinable terror which seized both of us whenever we passed by the door of a certain unfurnished room, in which we neither saw nor heard anything. And the strangest marvel of all was, that for once in my life I agreed with my wife, silly woman though she be—and allowed, after the third night, that it was impossible to stay a fourth in that house. Accordingly, on the fourth morning I summoned the woman who kept the house and attended on us, and told her that the rooms did not quite suit us, and we would not stay out our week. She said, dryly: 'I know why; you have stayed longer than any other lodger. Few ever stayed a second night; none before you a third. But I take it they have been very kind to you.'

"'They—who?' I asked, affecting to smile.

"'Why, they who haunt the house, whoever they are. I don't mind them; I remember them many years ago, when I lived in this house, not as a servant; but I know they will be the death of me some day. I don't care—I'm old, and must die soon anyhow; and then I shall be with them, and in this house still.' The woman spoke with so dreary a calmness, that really it was a sort of awe that prevented my conversing with her further. I paid for my week, and too happy were my wife and I to get off so cheaply."

"You excite my curiosity," said I; "nothing I should like better than to sleep in a haunted house. Pray give me the address of the one which you left so ignominiously."

My friend gave me the address; and when we parted, I walked straight towards the house thus indicated.

It is situated on the north side of Oxford Street, in a dull but respectable thoroughfare. I found the house shut up—no bill at the window, and no response to my knock. As I was turning away, a beer-boy, collecting pewter pots at the neighbouring areas, said to me, "Do you want any one at that house, sir?"

"Yes, I heard it was to be let."

"Let!—why, the woman who kept it is dead—has been dead these three weeks, and no one can be found to stay there, though Mr. J—— offered ever so much. He offered mother, who chars for him, £1 a week just to open and shut the windows, and she would not."

"Would not!—and why?"

"The house is haunted; and the old woman who kept it was found dead in her bed, with her eyes wide open. They say the devil strangled her."

"Pooh!—you speak of Mr. J——. Is he the owner of the house?"

"Yes."

"Where does he live?"

"in G——Street, No.—."

"What is he?—in any business?"

"No, sir—nothing particular; a single gentleman."

I gave the pot-boy the gratuity earned by his liberal information, and proceeded to Mr. J——, in G—— Street, which was close by the street that boasted the haunted house. I was lucky enough to find Mr. J—— at home—an elderly man, with intelligent countenance and prepossessing manners.

I communicated my name and my business frankly. I said I heard the house was considered to be haunted—that I had a strong desire to examine a house with so equivocal a reputation—that I should be greatly obliged if he would allow me to hire it, though only for a night. I was willing to pay for that privilege whatever he might be inclined to ask. "Sir," said Mr. J——, with great courtesy, "the house is at your service, for as short or as long a time as you please. Rent is out of the question—the obligation will be on my side should you be able to discover the cause of the strange phenomena which at present deprive it of all value. I cannot let it, for I cannot even get a servant to keep it in order or answer the door. Unluckily the house is haunted, if I may use that expression, not only by night, but by day; though at night the disturbances are of a more unpleasant and sometimes of a more alarming character. The poor old woman who died in it three weeks ago was a pauper whom I took out of a workhouse, for in her childhood she had been known to some of my family, and had once been in such good circumstance that she had rented that house of my uncle. She was a woman of superior education and strong mind, and was the only person I could ever induce to remain in the house. Indeed, since her death, which was sudden, and the coroner's inquest, which gave it notoriety in the neighbourhood, I have so despaired of finding any person to take charge of the house, much more a tenant, that I would willingly let it rent free for a year to any one who would pay its rates and taxes."

"How long is it since the house acquired this sinister character?"

"That I can scarcely tell you, but very many years since. The old woman I spoke of said it was haunted when she rented it between thirty and forty years ago. The fact is, that my life has been spent in the East Indies, and in the civil service of the Company. I returned to England last year, on inheriting the fortune of an uncle, among whose possessions was the house in question. I found it shut up and uninhabited. I was told that it was haunted, that no one would inhabit it. I smiled at what seemed to me so idle a story. I spent some money in repairing it—added to its old-fashioned furniture a few modern articles—advertised it, and obtained a lodger for a year. He was a colonel on half-pay. He came in with his family, a son and a daughter, and four or five servants: they all left the house the next day; and, although each of them declared that he had seen something different from that which had scared the others, a something still was equally terrible to all. I really could not in conscience sue, nor even blame, the colonel for breach of agreement. Then I put in the old woman I have spoken of, and she was empowered to let the house in apartments. I never had one lodger who stayed more than three days. I do not tell you their stories—to no two lodgers have there been exactly the same phenomena repeated. It is better that you should judge for yourself, than enter the house with an imagination influenced by previous narratives; only be prepared to see and to hear something or other, and take whatever precautions you yourself please."

"Have you never had a curiosity yourself to pass a night in that house?"

"Yes. I passed not a night but three hours in broad daylight alone in that house. My curiosity is not satisfied, but it is quenched. I have no desire to renew the experiment. You cannot complain, you see, sir, that I am not sufficiently candid; and unless your interest be exceedingly eager and your nerves unusually strong, I honestly add, that I advise you not to pass a night in that house."

"My interest is exceedingly keen," said I, "and though only a coward will boast of his nerves in situations wholly unfamiliar to him, yet my nerves have been seasoned in such variety of danger that I have the right to rely on them—even in a haunted house."

Mr J—— said very little more; he took the keys of the house out of his bureau, gave them to me,—and, thanking him cordially for his frankness, and his urbane concession to my wish, I carried off my prize.

Impatient for the experiment, as soon as I reached home, I summoned my confidential servant—a young man of gay spirits, fearless temper, and as free from superstitious prejudice as any one I could think of.

"F——," said I, "you remember in Germany how disappointed we were at not finding a ghost in that old castle, which was said to be haunted by a headless apparition? Well, I have heard of a house in London which, I have reason to hope, is decidedly haunted. I mean to sleep there to-night. From what I hear, there is no doubt that something will allow itself to be seen or to be heard— something, perhaps, excessively horrible. Do you think, if I take you with me, I may rely on your presence of mind, whatever may happen?"

"Oh, sir! pray trust me" answered F——, grinning with delight.

"Very well; then here are the keys of the house—this is the address. Go now, —select for me any bedroom you please; and since the house has not been inhabited for weeks, make up a good fire—air the bed well—see, of course, that there are candles as well as fuel. Take with you my revolver and my dagger—so much for my weapons—arm yourself equally well; and if we are not a match for a dozen ghosts, we shall be but a sorry couple of Englishmen."

I was engaged for the rest of the day on business so urgent that I had not leisure to think much on the nocturnal adventure to which I had plighted my honour. I dined alone, and very late, and while dining, read, as is my habit. I selected one of the volumes of Macaulay's essays. I thought to myself that I would take the book with me; there was so much of healthfulness in the style, and practical life in the subjects, that it would serve as a antidote against the influences of superstitious fancy.

Accordingly, about half-past nine, I put the book into my pocket, and strolled leisurely towards the haunted house. I took with me a favourite dog,—an exceedingly sharp, bold, and vigilant bull-terrier, a dog fond of prowling about strange ghostly corners and passages at night in search of rats—a dog of dogs for a ghost.

It was a summer night, but chilly, the sky somewhat gloomy and overcast. Still there was a moon—faint and sickly, but still a moon—and if the clouds permitted, after midnight it would be brighter.

I reached the house, knocked, and my servant opened with a cheerful smile.

"All right, sir, and very comfortable."

"Oh!" said I, rather disappointed; "have you not seen nor heard anything remarkable?"

"Well, sir, I must own I have heard something queer."

"What?—what?"

"The sound of feet pattering behind me; and once or twice small noises like whispers close at my ear—nothing more."

"You are not at all frightened?"

"I, not a bit of it, sir;" and the man's bold look reassured me on one point—viz., that happen what might, he would not desert me.

We were in the hall, the street-door closed, and my attention was now drawn to my dog. He had at first run in eagerly enough, but had sneaked back to the door, and was scratching and whining to get out. After patting him on the head, and encouraging him gently, the dog seemed to reconcile himself to the situation, and followed me and F—— through the house, but keeping close at my heels instead of hurrying inquisitively in advance, which was his usual and normal habit in all strange places. We first visited the subterranean apartments, the kitchen and other offices, and especially the cellars, in which last there were two or three bottles of wine still left in a bin, covered with cobwebs, and evidently, by their appearance, undisturbed for many years. It was clear that the ghosts were not wine-bibbers. For the rest we discovered nothing of interest. There was a gloomy little back-yard, with very high walls. The stones of this yard were very damp; and what with the damp, and what with the dust and smoke-grime on the pavement, our feet left a slight impression where we passed. And now appeared the first strange phenomenon witnessed by myself in this strange abode. I saw, just before me, the print of a foot suddenly form itself, as it were. I stopped, caught hold of my servant, and pointed to it. In advance of that footprint as suddenly dropped another. We both saw it. I advanced quickly to the place; the footprint kept advancing before me, a small footprint; the foot of a child: the impression was too faint thoroughly to distinguish the shape, but it seemed to us both that it was the print of a naked foot. This phenomenon ceased when we arrived at the opposite wall, nor did it repeat itself on returning. We remounted the stairs, and entered the rooms on the ground floor, a dining parlour, a small back parlour, and a still smaller third room that had been probably appropriated to a footman—all still as death. We then visited the drawing-rooms, which seemed fresh and new. In the front room I seated myself in an arm-chair. F—— placed on the table the candlestick with which he had lighted us. I told him to shut the door. As he turned to do so, a chair opposite to me moved from the wall quickly and noiselessly, and dropped itself about a yard from my own chair, immediately fronting it.

"Why, this is better than the turning-tables," said I, with a half-laugh; and as I laughed, my dog put back his head and howled.

F——, coming back, had not observed the movement of the chair. He employed himself now in stilling the dog. I continued to gaze on the chair, and fancied I saw on it a pale blue misty outline of a human figure, but an outline so indistinct that I could only distrust my own vision. The dog now was quiet.

"Put back that chair opposite to me" said I to F——; "put it back to the wall."

F—— obeyed. "Was that you, sir," said he, turning abruptly.

"I!—what?"

"Why, something struck me. I felt it sharply on the shoulder—just here."

"No," said I. "But we have jugglers present, and though we may not discover their tricks, we shall catch *them* before they frighten *us*."

We did not stay long in the drawing-rooms—in fact, they felt

140

so damp and so chilly that I was glad to get to the fire upstairs. We locked the doors of the drawing-rooms—a precaution which, I should observe, we had taken with all the rooms we had searched below. The bedroom my servant had selected for me was the best on the floor—a large one, with two windows fronting the street. The four-posted bed, which took up no inconsiderable space, was opposite to the fire, which burnt clear and bright; a door in the wall to the left, between the bed and the window, communicated with the room which my servant appropriated to himself. This last was a small room with a sofa-bed, and had no communication with the landing-place—no other door but that which conducted to the bedroom I was to occupy. On either side of my fireplace was a cupboard, without locks, flush with the wall, and covered with the same dull-brown paper. We examined these cupboards—only hooks to suspend female dresses—nothing else; we sounded the walls—evidently solid—the outer walls of the building. Having finished the survey of these apartments, warmed myself a few moments, and lighted my cigar, I then, still accompanied by F——, went forth to complete my reconnoitre. In the landing-place there was another door; it was closed firmly. "Sir," said my servant, in surprise, "I unlocked this door with all the others when I first came; it cannot have got locked from the inside, for——"

Before he had finished his sentence, the door, which neither of us then was touching, opened quietly of itself. We looked at each other a single instant. The same thought seized both—some human agency might be detected here. I rushed in first, my servant followed. A small blank dreary room without furniture—a few empty boxes and hampers in a corner—small window—the shutters closed—not even a fireplace—no other door but that by which we had entered—no carpet on the floor, and the floor seemed very old, uneven, work-eaten, mended here and there, as was shown by the whiter patches on the wood; but no living being, and no visible place in which a living being could have hidden. As we stood gazing round, the door by which we had entered closed as quietly as it had before opened: we were imprisoned.

For the first time I felt a creep of undefinable horror. Not so my servant. "Why, they don't think to trap us, sir; I could break that trumpery door with a kick of my foot."

"Try first if it will open to your hand," said I, shaking off the vague apprehension that had seized me, "while I unclose the shutters and see what is without."

I unbarred the shutters—the window looked on the little back-yard I have before described; there was no ledge without—nothing to break the sheer descent of the wall. No man getting out of that window would have found any footing till he had fallen on the stones below.

F——, meanwhile, was vainly attempting to open the door. He now turned round to me and asked my permission to use force. And I should here state, in justice to the servant, that, far from evincing any superstitious terrors, his nerve, composure, and even gaiety amidst circumstances so extraordinary, compelled my admiration, and made me congratulate myself on having secured a companion in every way fitted to the occasion. I willingly gave him the permission he required. But though he was a remarkably strong man, his force was as idle as his milder efforts; the door did not even shake to his stoutest kick. Breathless and panting, he desisted. I then tried the door myself, equally in vain. As I ceased from the effort, again that creep of horror came over me; but this time it was more cold and stubborn. I felt as if some strange and ghastly exhalation were rising up from the chinks of that rugged floor, and filling the atmosphere with a venomous influence hostile to human life. The door now very slowly and quietly opened as of its own accord. We precipitated ourselves into the landing-place. We both saw a large pale light—as large as the human figure, but shapeless and unsubstantial—move before us, and ascend the stairs that led from the landing into the attics. I followed the light, and my servant followed me. It entered to the right of the landing, a small garret, of which the door stood open. I entered in the same instant. The light then collapsed into a small globule, exceedingly brilliant and vivid: rested a moment on a bed in the corner, quivered, and vanished. We approached the bed and examined it—a half-tester, such as is commonly found in attics devoted to servants. On the drawers that stood near it we perceived an old faded silk kerchief, with the needle still left in a rent half repaired. The kerchief was covered with dust; probably it had belonged to the old woman who had last died in that house, and this might have been her sleeping room. I had sufficient curiosity to open the drawers: there were a few odds and ends of female dress, and two letters tied round with a narrow ribbon of faded yellow. I took the liberty to possess myself of the letters. We found nothing else in the room worth noticing—nor did the light reappear; but we distinctly heard, as we turned to go, a pattering footfall on the floor—just before us. We went through the other attics (in all four), the footfall still preceding us. Nothing to be seen—nothing but the footfall heard. I had the letters in my hand: just as I was descending the stairs I distinctly felt my wrist seized, and a faint soft effort made to draw the letters from my clasp. I only held them the more tightly, and the effort ceased.

We regained the bed-chamber appropriated to myself, and I then remarked that my dog had not followed us when we had left it. He was thrusting himself close to the fire, and trembling. I was impatient to examine the letters; and while I read them, my servant opened a little box in which he had deposited the weapons I had ordered him to bring; took them out, placed them on a table close at my bed-head, and then occupied himself in soothing the dog, who, however, seemed to heed him very little.

The letters were short—they were dated; the dates exactly thirty-five years ago. They were evidently from a lover to his mistress, or a husband to some young wife. Not only the terms of expression, but a distinct reference to a former voyage, indicated the writer to have been a seafarer. The spelling and handwriting were those of a man imperfectly educated, but still the language itself was forcible. In the expressions of endearment there was a kind of rough wild love; but here and there were dark unintelligible hints at some secret not of love—some secret that seemed of crime. "We ought to love each other," was one of the sentences I remember, "for how, every one else would execrate us if all was known." Again: "Don't let any one be in the same room with you at night—you talk in your sleep." And again: "What's done can't be undone; and I tell you there's nothing against us unless the dead could come to life." Here there was underlined in a better handwriting (a female's), "They do!" At the end of the letter latest in date the same female hand had written these words: "Lost at sea the 4th of June the same day as ——."

I put down the letters, and began to muse over their contents.

Fearing, however, that the train of thought into which I fell might unsteady my nerves, I fully determined to keep my mind in a fit state to cope with whatever of marvellous the advancing night might bring forth. I roused myself—laid the letters on the table— stirred up the fire, which was still bright and cheering, and opened my volume of Macaulay. I read quietly enough till about half-past eleven. I then threw myself dressed upon the bed, and told my servant he might retire to his own room, but must keep himself awake. I bade him leave open the door between the two rooms. Thus alone, I kept two candles burning on the table by my bed-head. I placed my watch beside the weapons, and calmly resumed my Macaulay. Opposite to me the fire burned clear; and on the hearth-rug, seemingly asleep, lay the dog. In about twenty minutes I felt an exceedingly cold air pass by my cheek, like a sudden draught. I fancied the door to my right, communicating with the landing-place, must have got open; but no—it was closed. I then turned my glance to my left, and saw the flame of the candles violently swayed as by a wind. At the same moment the watch beside the revolver softly slid from the table—softly, softly—no visible hand—it was gone. I sprang up, seizing the revolver with the one hand, the dagger with the other: I was not willing that my weapons should share the fate of the watch. Thus armed, I looked round the floor—no sign of the watch. Three slow, loud, distinct knocks were now heard at the bed-head; my servant called out, "Is that you, sir?"

"No; be on your guard."

The dog now roused himself and sat on his haunches, his ears moving quickly backwards and forwards. He kept his eyes fixed on me with a look so strange that he concentred all my attention on himself. Slowly, he rose up, all his hair bristling, and stood perfectly rigid, and with the same wild stare. I had no time, however, to examine the dog. Presently my servant emerged from his room; and if ever I saw horror in the human face, it was then. I should not have recognised him had we met in the street, so altered was every lineament. He passed by me quickly, saying in a whisper that seemed scarcely to come from his lip, "Run—run! it is after me!" He gained the door to the landing, pulled it open, and rushed forth. I followed him into the landing involuntarily, calling him to stop; but, without heeding me, he bounded down the stairs, clinging to the balusters, and taking several steps at a time. I heard, where I stood, the street-door open—heard it again clap to. I was left alone in the haunted house.

It was but for a moment that I remained undecided whether or not to follow my servant; pride and curiosity alike forbade so dastardly a flight. I re-entered my room, closing the door after me, and proceeded cautiously into the interior chamber. I encountered nothing to justify my servant's terror. I again carefully examined the walls, to see if there were any concealed door. I could find no trace of one—not even a seam in the dull-brown paper with which the room was hung. How, then, had the THING, whatever it was, which had so scared him, obtained ingress except through my own chamber?

I returned to my room, shut and locked the door that opened upon the interior one, and stood on the hearth, expectant and prepared. I now perceived that the dog had slunk into an angle of the wall, and was pressing himself close against it, as if literally striving to force his way into it. I approached the animal and spoke to it; the poor brute was evidently beside itself with terror. It showed all its teeth, the slaver dropping from its jaws, and would certainly have bitten me if I had touched it. It did not seem to recognise me. Whoever has seen at the Zoological Gardens a rabbit, fascinated by a serpent, cowering in a corner, may form some idea of the anguish which the dog exhibited. Finding all efforts to soothe the animal in vain, and fearing that his bite might be as venomous in that state as in the madness of hydrophobia, I left him alone, placed my weapons on the table beside the fire, seated myself, and recommenced my Macaulay.

Perhaps, in order to appear seeking credit for a courage, or rather a coolness which the reader may conceive I exaggerate, I may be pardoned if I pause to indulge in one or two egotistical remarks.

As I hold presence of mind, or what is called courage, to be precisely proportioned to familiarity with the circumstances that lead to it, so I should say that I had been long sufficiently familiar with all experiments that appertain to the Marvellous. I had witnessed many very extraordinary phenomena in various parts of the world—phenomena that would be either totally disbelieved if I stated them, or ascribed to supernatural agencies. Now, my theory is that the Supernatural is the Impossible, and that what is called supernatural is only a something in the laws of nature of which we have been hitherto ignorant. Therefore, if a ghost rise before me, I have not the right to say, "So, then, the supernatural is possible," but rather, "So, then, the apparition of a ghost is, contrary to received opinion, within the laws of nature—*i.e.,* not supernatural."

Now, in all that I had hitherto witnessed, and indeed in all the wonders which the amateurs of mystery in our age record as facts, a material living agency is always required. On the Continent you will find still magicians who assert that they can raise spirits. Assume for the moment that they assert truly, still the living material form of the magician is present; and he is the material agency by which, from some constitutional peculiarities, certain strange phenomena are represented to your natural senses.

Accept, again, as truthful, the tales of Spirit Manifestation in America—musical or other sounds—writings on paper, produced by no discernible hand—articles of furniture moved without apparent human agency—or the actual sight and touch of hands, to which no bodies seem to belong—still there must be found the MEDIUM or living being, with constitutional peculiarities capable of obtaining these signs. In fine, in all such marvels, supposing even that there is no imposture, there must be a human being like ourselves by whom, or through whom, the effects presented to human beings are produced. It is so with the now familiar phenomena of mesmerism or electro-biology; the mind of the person operated on is affected through a material living agent. Nor, supposing it true that a mesmerised patient can respond to the will or passes of a mesmeriser a hundred miles distant, is the response less occasioned by a material being; it may be through a material fluid—call it Electric, call it Odic, call it what you will—which as the power of traversing space and passing obstacles, that the material effect is communicated from one to the other. Hence all that I had hitherto witnessed, or expected to witness, in this strange house, I believed to be occasioned through some agency or medium as mortal as myself; and this idea necessarily prevented the awe with which those who regard as supernatural things that are not within the ordinary operations of nature, might have been impressed by the adventures of that memorable night.

As, then, it was my conjecture that all that was presented, or would be presented to my senses, must originate is some human being gifted by constitution with the power so to present them and having some motive so to do, I felt an interest in my theory which, in its way, was rather philosophical than superstitious. And I can sincerely say that I was in as tranquil a temper for observation as any practical experimentalist could be in awaiting the effects of some rare, though perhaps perilous, chemical combination. Of course, the more I kept my mind detached from fancy, the more the temper fitted for observation would be obtained; and I therefore riveted eye and thought on the strong daylight sense in the page of my Macaulay.

I now became aware that something interposed between the page and the light—the page was overshadowed: I looked up, and I saw what I shall find it very difficult, perhaps impossible to describe.

It was a Darkness shaping itself forth from the air in very undefined outline. I cannot say it was of a human form, and yet it had more resemblance to a human form, or rather shadow, than to anything else. As it stood, wholly apart and distinct from the air and the light around it, its dimensions seemed gigantic, the summit nearly touching the ceiling. While I gazed, a feeling of intense cold seized me. An iceberg before me could not more have chilled me; nor could the cold of an iceberg have been more purely physical. I feel convinced that it was not the cold caused by fear. As I continued to gaze, I thought—but this I cannot say with precision—that I distinguished two eyes looking on me from the height. One moment I fancied that I distinguished them clearly, the next they seemed gone; but still two rays of a pale-blue light frequently shot through the darkness, as from the height on which I half believed, half doubted, that I had encountered the eyes.

I strove to speak—my voice utterly failed me; I could only think to myself, "Is this fear? it is not fear!" I strove to rise in vain; I felt as if weighed down by an irresistible force. Indeed, my impression was that of an immense and overwhelming Power opposed to my volition;—that sense of utter inadequacy to cope with a force beyond man's, which one may feel *physically* in a storm at sea, in a conflagration, or when confronting some wild beast, or rather, perhaps, the shark of the ocean, I felt *morally*. Opposed to my will was another will, as far superior to its strength as storm, fire, and shark are superior in material force to the force of man.

And now, as this impression grew on me—now came, at last, horror—horror to a degree that no words can convey. Still I retained pride, if not courage; and in my own mind I said, "This is horror, but it is not fear, unless I fear I cannot be harmed; my reason rejects this thing; it is an illusion—I do not fear." With a violent effort I succeeded at last in stretching out my hand towards the weapon on the table: as I did so, on the arm and shoulder I received a strange shock, and my arm fell to my side powerless. And now, to add to my horror, the light began slowly to wane from the candles—they were not, as it were, extinguished, but their flame seemed very gradually withdrawn: it was the same with the fire—the light was extracted from the fuel; in a few minutes the room was in utter darkness. The dread that came over me, to be thus in the dark with that dark Thing, whose power was so intensely felt, brought a reaction of nerve. In fact, terror had reached that climax, that either my senses must have deserted me, or I must have burst through the spell. I did burst through it. I found voice, though the voice was a shriek. I remember that I broke forth with words like these: "I do not fear, my soul does not fear;" and at the same time I found strength to rise. Still in that profound gloom I rushed to one of the windows—tore aside the curtain—flung open the shutters; my first thought was—LIGHT. And when I saw the moon high, clear, and calm, I felt a joy that almost compensated for the previous terror. There was the moon, there was also the light from the gas-lamps in the deserted slumberous street. I turned to look back into the room; the moon penetrated its shadow very palely and partially—but still there was light. The dark Thing, whatever it might be, was gone—except that I could yet see a dim shadow, which seemed the shadow of that shade, against the opposite wall.

My eye now rested on the table, and from under the table (which was without cloth or cover—an old mahogany round table) there rose a hand, visible as far as the wrist. It was a hand, seemingly, as much of flesh and blood as my own, but the hand of an aged person—lean, wrinkled, small too—a woman's hand. That hand very softly closed on the two letters that lay on the table: hand and letters both vanished. There then came the same three loud measured knocks I had heard at the bed-head before this extraordinary drama had commenced.

As those sounds slowly ceased, I felt the whole room vibrate sensibly; and at the far end there rose, as from the floor, sparks or globules like bubbles of light, many-coloured—green, yellow, fire-red, azure. Up and down, to and fro, hither, thither, as tiny Will-o'-the-Wisps, the sparks moved, slow or swift, each at its own caprice. A chair (as in the drawing-room below) was now advanced from the wall without apparent agency, and placed at the opposite side of the table. Suddenly, as forth from the chair, there grew a shape—a woman's shape. It was distinct as a shape of life—ghastly as a shape of death. The face was that of youth, with a strange mournful beauty; the throat and shoulders were bare, the rest of the form in a loose robe of cloudy white. It began sleeking its long yellow hair, which fell over its shoulders; its eyes were not turned towards me, but to the door; it seemed listening, watching, waiting. The shadow of the shade in the background grew darker; and again

I thought I beheld the eyes gleaming out from the summit of the shadow—eyes fixed upon that shape.

As if from the door, though it did not open, there grew out another shape, equally distinct, equally ghastly—a man's shape—a young man's. It was in the dress of the last century, or rather in a likeness of such dress (for both the male shape and the female, though defined, were evidently unsubstantial, impalpable—simulacra—phantasms); and there was something incongruous, grotesque, yet fearful, in the contrast between the elaborate finery, the courtly precision of that old-fashioned garb, with its ruffles and lace and buckles, and the corpse-like aspect and ghost-like stillness of the flitting wearer. Just as the male shape approached the female, the dark Shadow started from the wall, all three for a moment wrapped in darkness. When the pale light returned, the two phantoms were as if in the grasp of the Shadow that towered between them; and there was a blood-stain on the breast of the female; and the phantom male was leaning on its phantom sword, and blood seemed trickling fast from the ruffles, from the lace; and the darkness of the intermediate Shadow swallowed them up—they were gone. And again the bubbles of light shot, and sailed, and undulated, growing thicker and thicker and more wildly confused in their movements.

The closet door to the right of the fireplace now opened, and from the aperture there came the form of an aged woman. In her hand she held letters,— the very letters over which I had seen *the* Hand close; and behind her I heard a footstep. She turned round as if to listen, and then she opened the letters and seemed to read; and over her shoulder I saw a livid face, the face as of a man long drowned—bloated, bleached—seaweed tangled in its dripping hair; and at her feet lay a form as of a corpse, and beside the corpse there cowered a child, a miserable squalid child, with famine in its cheeks and fear in its eyes. And as I looked in the old woman's face, the wrinkles and lines vanished, and it became a face of youth—hard-eyed, stony, but still youth; and the Shadow darted forth, and darkened over these phantoms as it had darkened over the last.

Nothing now was left but the Shadow, and on that my eyes were intently fixed, till again eyes grew out of the Shadow-malignant, serpent eyes. And the bubbles of light again rose and fell, and in their disordered, irregular, turbulent maze, mingled with the wan moonlight. And now from these globules themselves, as from the shell of an egg, monstrous things burst out; the air grew filled with them; larvæ so bloodless and so hideous that I can in no way describe them except to remind the reader of the swarming life which the solar microscope brings before his eyes in a drop of water—things transparent, supple, agile, chasing each other, devouring each other—forms like nought ever beheld by the naked eye. As the shapes were without symmetry, so their movements were without order. In their very vagrancies there was no sport; they came round me and round, thicker and faster and swifter, swarming over my head, crawling over my right arm, which was outstretched in involuntary command against all evil beings. Sometimes I felt myself touched, but not by them; invisible hands touched me. Once I felt the clutch as of cold soft fingers at my throat. I was still equally conscious that if I gave way to fear I should be in bodily peril; and I concentrated all my faculties in the single focus of resisting, stubborn will. And I turned my sight from the Shadow—above all, from those strange serpent eyes—eyes that had now become distinctly visible. For there, though in nought else around me, I was aware that there was a WILL, and a will of intense, creative, working evil, which might crush down my own.

The pale atmosphere in the room began now to redden as if in the air of some near conflagration. The larvæ grew lurid as things that live in fire. Again the room vibrated; again were heard the three measured knocks; and again all things were swallowed up in the darkness of the dark Shadow, as if out of that darkness all had come, into that darkness all returned.

As the gloom receded, the Shadow was wholly gone. Slowly, as it had been withdrawn, the flame grew again into the candles on the table, again into the fuel in the grate. The whole room came once more calmly, healthfully into sight.

The two doors were still closed, the door communicating with the servant's room still locked. In the corner of the wall, into which he had so convulsively niched himself, lay the dog. I called to him—no movement; I approached—the animal was dead; his eyes protruded; his tongue out of his mouth; the froth gathered round his jaws. I took him in my arms; I brought him to the fire; I felt acute grief for the loss of my poor favourite—acute self-reproach; I accused myself of his death; I imagined he had died of fright. But what was my surprise on finding that his neck was actually broken. Had this been done in the dark?—must it not have been by a hand human as mine?—must there not have been a human agency all the while in that room? Good cause to suspect it. I cannot tell. I cannot do more than state the fact fairly; the reader may draw his own inference.

Another surprising circumstance—my watch was restored to the table from which it had been so mysteriously withdrawn; but it had stopped at the very moment it was so withdrawn; nor, despite all the skill of the watchmaker, has it ever gone since—that is, it will go in a strange erratic way for a few hours, and then come to a dead stop—it is worthless.

Nothing more chanced for the rest of the night. Nor, indeed, had I long to wait before the dawn broke. Nor till it was broad daylight did I quit the haunted house. Before I did so, I revisited the little blind room in which my servant and myself had been for a time imprisoned. I had a strong impression—for which I could not account—that from that room had originated the mechanism of the phenomena—if I may use the term—which had been experienced in my chamber. And though I entered it now in the clear day, with the sun peering through the filmy window, I still felt, as I stood on its floors, the creep of the horror which I had first there experienced the night before, and which had been so aggravated by what had passed in my own chamber. I could not, indeed, bear to stay more than half a minute within those walls. I descended the stairs, and again I heard the footfall before me; and when I opened the street door, I thought I could distinguish a very low laugh. I gained my own home, expecting to find my run-away servant there. But he had not presented himself, nor did I hear more of him for three days, when I received a letter from him, dated from Liverpool to this effect:

"HONOURED SIR:—I humbly entreat your pardon, though I can scarcely hope that you will think that I deserve it, unless—which Heaven forbid!—you saw what I did. I feel that it will be years before I can recover myself; and as to being fit for service, it is out of the question. I am therefore going to my brother-in-law at Melbourne. The ship sails tomorrow. Perhaps the long voyage may set me up. I do nothing now but start and tremble, and fancy IT is behind me. I humbly beg you, honoured sir, to order my clothes, and whatever wages are due to me, to be sent to my mother's, at Walworth—John knows her address."

The letter ended with additional apologies, somewhat incoherent, and explanatory details as to effects that had been under the writer's charge.

This flight may perhaps warrant a suspicion that the man

wished to go to Australia, and had been somehow or other fraudulently mixed up with the events of the night. I say nothing in refutation of that conjecture; rather, I suggest it as one that would seem to many persons the most probable solution of improbable occurrences. My belief in my own theory remained unshaken. I returned in the evening to the house, to bring away in a hack cab the things I had left there, with my poor dog's body. In this task I was not disturbed, nor did any incident worth note befall me, except that still, on ascending and descending the stairs, I heard the same footfall in advance. On leaving the house, I went to Mr. J——'s. He was at home. I returned him the keys, told him that my curiosity was sufficiently gratified, and was about to relate quickly what had passed, when he stopped me, and said, though with much politeness, that he had no longer any interest in a mystery which none had ever solved.

I determined at least to tell him of the two letters I had read, as well as the extraordinary manner in which they had disappeared, and I then inquired if he thought they had been addressed to the woman who had died in the house, and if there were anything in her early history which could possibly confirm the dark suspicions to which the letters gave rise. Mr. J—— seemed startled, and, after musing a few moments, answered: "I am but little acquainted with the woman's earlier history, except, as I before told you, that her family were known to mine. But you revive some vague reminiscences to her prejudice. I will make inquiries, and inform you of their result. Still, even if we could admit the popular superstition that a person who had been either the perpetrator or the victim of dark crimes in life could revisit, as a restless spirit, the scene in which those crimes had been committed, I should observe that the house was infested by strange sights and sounds before the old woman died—you smile—what would you say?"

"I would say this, that I am convinced, if we could get to the bottom of these mysteries, we should find a living human agency."

"What! you believe it is all an imposture? for what object?"

"Not an imposture in the ordinary sense of the word. If suddenly I were to sink into a deep sleep, from which you could not awake me, but in that sleep could answer questions with an accuracy which I could not pretend to when awake—tell you what money you had in your pocket—nay, describe your very thoughts—it is not necessarily an imposture, any more than it is necessarily supernatural. I should be, unconsciously to myself,

152

under a mesmeric influence, conveyed to me from a distance by a human being who had acquired power over me by previous *rapport.*"

"But if a mesmeriser could so affect another living being, can you suppose that a mesmeriser could also affect inanimate objects: move chairs—open and shut doors?"

"Or impress our senses with the belief in such effects—we never having been *en rapport* with the person acting on us? No. What is commonly called mesmerism could not do this; but there may be a power akin to mesmerism and superior to it—the power that in the old days was called Magic. That such a power may extend to all inanimate objects of matter, I do not say; but if so, it would not be against nature—it would only be a rare power in nature which might be given to constitutions with certain peculiarities, and cultivated by practice to an extraordinary degree. That such a power might extend over the dead—that is, over certain thoughts and memories that the dead may still retain—and compel, not that which ought properly to be called the SOUL, and which is far beyond human reach, but rather a phantom of what has been most earth-stained on earth to make itself apparent to our senses—is a very ancient though obsolete theory, upon which I will hazard no opinion. But I do not conceive the power would be supernatural. Let me illustrate what I mean from an experiment which Paracelsus[1] describes as not difficult, and which the author of the *Curiosities of Literature* cites as credible: A flower perishes; you burn it. Whatever were the elements of that flower while it lived are gone, dispersed, you know not whither; you can never discover nor re-collect them. But you can by chemistry, out of the burnt dust of that flower, raise a spectrum of the flower, just as it seemed in life. It may be the same with the human being. The soul has as much escaped you as the essence or elements of the flower. Still you may make a spectrum of it. And this phantom, though in the popular superstition it is held to be the soul of the departed, must not be confounded with the true soul; it is but the eidolon of the dead form. Hence, like the best attested stories of ghosts or spirits, the thing that most strikes us is the absence of what we hold to be the soul; that is, of superior emancipated intelligence. These apparitions come for little or no object—they seldom speak when they do come; if they speak, they utter no ideas above those of an ordinary person on earth. American spirit-seers have published volumes of communications, in prose and verse, which they assert to be given in the names of the most illustrious dead—Shakespeare, Bacon—heaven knows whom. Those communications, taking the best, are certainly not a whit of higher order than would be communications from living persons of fair talent and education; they are wondrously inferior to what Bacon, Shakespeare, and Plato said and wrote when on earth. Nor, what is more noticeable, do they ever contain an idea that was not on the earth before. Wonderful, therefore, as such phenomena may be (granting them to be truthful), I see much that philosophy may question, nothing that it is incumbent on philosophy to deny—viz., nothing supernatural. They are but ideas conveyed somehow or other (we have not yet discovered the means) from one mortal brain to another. Whether, in so doing, tables walk of their own accord, or fiendlike shapes appear in a magic circle, or bodyless hands rise and remove material objects, or a Thing of Darkness, such as presented itself to me, freeze our blood—still am I persuaded that these are but agencies conveyed, as by electric wires, to my own brain from the brain of another. In some constitutions there is a natural chemistry, and those constitutions may produce chemic wonders—in others a natural fluid, call it electricity, and these may produce electric wonders. But the wonders differ from Normal Science in this—they are alike objectless, purposeless, puerile, frivolous. They lead on to no grand results; and therefore the world does not heed, and true sages have not cultivated them. But sure I am, that of all I saw or heard, a man, human as myself, was the remote originator; and I believe unconsciously to himself as to the exact effects produced, for this reason: no two persons, you say, have ever told you that they experienced exactly the same thing. Well, observe, no two persons ever experience exactly the same dream. If this were an ordinary imposture, the machinery would be arranged for results that would but little vary; if it were a supernatural agency permitted by the Almighty, it would surely be for some definite end. These phenomena belong to neither class; my persuasion is that they originate in some brain now far distant; that that brain had no distinct volition in anything that occurred; that what does occur reflects but its devious, motley, ever-shifting, half-formed thoughts; in short, that it has been but the dreams of such a brain put into action and invested with a semi-substance. That this brain is of immense power, that it can set matter into movement, that it is malignant and destructive, I believe; some material force must have killed my dog; the same force might, for aught I know, have sufficed to kill myself, had I been as subjugated by terror as the dog—had my intellect or my spirit given me no countervailing resistance in my will."

"It killed your dog! that is fearful! indeed it is strange that no animal can be induced to stay in that house; not even a cat. Rats and mice are never found in it."

"The instincts of the brute creation detect influences deadly to their existence. Man's reason has a sense less subtle, because it has a resisting power more supreme. But enough; do you comprehend my theory?"

"Yes, though imperfectly—and I accept any crotchet (pardon the word), however odd, rather than embrace at once the notion of ghosts and hobgoblins we imbibed in our nurseries. Still, to my unfortunate house the evil is the same. What on earth can I do with the house?"

"I will tell you what I would do. I am convinced from my own internal feelings that the small unfurnished room at right angles to the door of the bedroom which I occupied forms a starting-point or receptacle for the influences which haunt the house; and I strongly advise you to have the walls opened, the floor removed— nay, the whole room pulled down. I observe that it is detached from the body of the house, built over the small back-yard, and could be removed without injury to the rest of the building."

"And you think, if I did that——"

"You would cut off the telegraph wires. Try it. I am so persuaded that I am right, that I will pay half the expense if you will allow me to direct the operations."

"Nay, I am well able to afford the costs; for the rest, allow me to write to you."

About ten days after I received a letter from Mr. J——, telling me that he had visited the house since I had seen him; that he had found the two letters I had described, replaced in the drawer from which I had taken them; that he had read them with misgivings like my own; that he had instituted a cautious inquiry about the woman to whom I rightly conjectured they had been written. It seemed that thirty-six years ago (a year before the date of the letters) she had married, against the wish of her relations, an American of very suspicious character; in fact, he was generally believed to have been a pirate. She herself was the daughter of very respectable tradespeople, and had served in a capacity of a nursery governess before her marriage. She had a brother, a widower, who was considered wealthy, and who had one child of about six years old. A month after the marriage, the body of this brother was found in the Thames, near London Bridge; there seemed some marks of violence about his throat, but they were not deemed sufficient to warrant the inquest in any other verdict than that of "found drowned".

The American and his wife took charge of the little boy, the deceased brother having by his will left his sister the guardian of his only child—and in event of the child's death, the sister inherited. The child died about six months afterwards—it was supposed to have been neglected and ill-treated. The neighbours deposed to have heard it shriek at night. The surgeon who had examined it after death said that it was emaciated as if from want of nourishment, and the body was covered with livid bruises. It seemed that one winter night the child had sought to escape— crept out into the back-yard—tried to scale the wall—fallen back exhausted, and been found at morning on the stones in a dying state. But though there was some evidence of cruelty, there was none of murder; and the aunt and her husband had sought to palliate cruelty by alleging the exceeding stubbornness and perversity of the child, who was declared to be half-witted. Be that as it may, at the orphan's death the aunt inherited her brother's fortune. Before the first wedded year was out, the American quitted England abruptly, and never returned to it. He obtained a cruising vessel, which was lost in the Atlantic two years afterwards. The widow was left in affluence: but reverses of various kinds had befallen her: a bank broke—an investment failed—she went into a small business and became insolvent— then she entered into service, sinking lower and lower, from housekeeper down to maid-of-all-work—never long retaining a place, though nothing decided against her character was ever alleged. She was considered sober, honest, and peculiarly quiet in her ways; still nothing prospered with her. And so she had dropped into the workhouse, from which Mr. J—— had taken her, to be placed in charge of the very house which she had rented as mistress in the first year of her wedded life.

Mr. J—— added that he had passed an hour alone in the unfurnished room which I had urged him to destroy, and that his impressions of dread while there were so great, though he had neither heard nor seen anything, that he was eager to have the walls bared and the floors removed as I had suggested. He had engaged persons for the work, and would commence any day I would name.

The day was accordingly fixed. I repaired to the haunted house—we went into the blind dreary room, took up the skirting, and then the floors. Under the rafters, covered with rubbish, was found a trap-door, quite large enough to admit a man. It was closely nailed down, with clamps and rivets of iron. On removing these we descended into a room below, the existence of which had never been suspected. In this room there had been a window and a flue, but they had been bricked over, evidently for many years. By the help of candles we examined this place; it still retained some mouldering furniture—three chairs, an oak settle, a table—all of the fashion of about eighty years ago. There was a chest of drawers against the wall, in which we found, half-rotted away, old-fashioned articles of a man's dress, such as might have been worn eighty or a hundred years ago by a gentleman of some rank—costly steel buckles and buttons, like those yet worn in court-dresses, a handsome court sword—in a waistcoat which had once been rich with gold-lace, but which was now blackened and foul with damp, we found five guineas, a few silver coins, and an ivory ticket, probably for some place of entertainment long since passed away. But our main discovery was in a kind of iron safe fixed to the wall, the lock of which it cost us much trouble to get picked.

In this safe were three shelves, and two small drawers. Ranged on the shelves were several small bottles of crystal, hermetically stopped. They contained colourless volatile essences, of the nature of which I shall only say that they were not poisons—phosphor and ammonia entered into some of them. There were also some very curious glass tubes, and a small pointed rod of iron, with a large lump of rock-crystal, and another of amber—also a loadstone of great power.

In one of the drawers we found a miniature portrait set in gold, and retaining the freshness of its colours most remarkably, considering the length of time it had probably been there. The portrait was that of a man who might be somewhat advanced in middle life, perhaps forty-seven or forty-eight.

It was a remarkable face—a most impressive face. If you could fancy some mighty serpent transformed into man, preserving in the human lineaments the old serpent type, you would have a better idea of that countenance than long descriptions can convey:

the width and flatness of frontal—the tapering elegance of contour disguising the strength of the deadly jaw—the long, large, terrible eye, glittering and green as the emerald—and withal a certain ruthless calm, as if from the consciousness of an immense power.

Mechanically I turned round the miniature to examine the back of it, and on the back was engraved a pentacle; in the middle of the pentacle a ladder, and the third step of the ladder was formed by the date 1765. Examining still more minutely, I detected a spring; this, on being pressed, opened the back of the miniature as a lid. Within-side the lid were engraved, "Marianna to thee—Be faithful in life and in death to ——." Here follows a name that I will not mention, but it was not unfamiliar to me. I had heard it spoken of by old men in my childhood as the name borne by a dazzling charlatan who had made a great sensation in London for a year or so, and had fled the country on the charge of a double murder within his own house—that of his mistress and his rival. I said nothing of this to Mr. J——, to whom reluctantly I resigned the miniature.

We had found no difficulty in opening the first drawer within the iron safe; we found great difficulty in opening the second: it was not locked, but it resisted all efforts, till we inserted in the chinks the edge of a chisel. When we had thus drawn it forth, we found a very singular apparatus in the nicest order. Upon a small thin book, or rather tablet, was placed a saucer of crystal; this saucer was filled with a clear liquid—on that liquid floated a kind of compass, with a needle shifting rapidly round; but instead of the usual points of a compass were seven strange characters, not very unlike those used by astrologers to denote the planets. A peculiar, but not strong nor displeasing odour, came from this drawer, which was lined with a wood that we afterwards discovered to be hazel. Whatever the cause of this odour, it produced a material effect on the nerves. We all felt it, even the two workmen who were in the room—a creeping tingling sensation from the tips of the fingers to the roots of the hair. Impatient to examine the tablet, I removed the saucer. As I did so the needle of the compass went round and round with exceeding swiftness, and I felt a shock that ran through my whole frame, so that I dropped the saucer on the floor. The liquid was spilt—the saucer was broken—the compass rolled to the end of the room—and at that instant the walls shook to and fro, as if a giant had swayed and rocked them.

The two workmen were so frightened that they ran up the

ladder by which we had descended from the trap-door; but seeing that nothing more happened, they were easily induced to return.

Meanwhile I had opened the tablet: it was bound in plain red leather, with a silver clasp; it contained but one sheet of thick vellum, and on that sheet were inscribed, within a double pentacle, words in old monkish Latin, which are literally to be translated thus: "On all that it can reach within these walls—sentient or inanimate, living or dead—as moves the needle, so work my will! Accursed be the house, and restless be the dwellers therein."

We found no more. Mr. J—— burnt the tablet and its anathema. He razed to the foundations the part of the building containing the secret room with the chamber over it. He had then the courage to inhabit the house himself for a month, and a quieter, better-conditioned house could not be found in all London. Subsequently he let it to advantage, and his tenant has made no complaints.

TEXT REFERENCES

THE NYMPH OF THE LURLEI BERG - A TALE

In Greek mythology, the Syrens or Sirens, were sea demons, half woman, half bird. They lived on rocky outcrops in the sea and with their enchanting music lured sailors to their deaths.

The *Odyssey* records two Sirens but later tradition recalls three or four. Apollodorus noted that one played the lyre, another the flute and the third sang. The tradition remained imbued in sailors' superstitions until the late Middle Ages.

1   **Certes:** an archaic term for 'I assure you', stemming from the Latin ad certas- 'for a certainty'.

2   The idea of a gigantic snake or dragon coiled around the centre of the world is an ancient one native to many mythologies. In Norse myth it is named Jormungard, the 'Midgard Serpent', who curled around the world, biting on his own tail.

3   **chace:** the contemporary spelling of chase.

4   Here Bulwer adds the following footnote to his manuscript: *On this part of the stream there is still an echo which repeats five times the sound hunting horn.*

THE FALLEN STAR; OR, THE HISTORY OF A FALSE RELIGION

This story, along with The Life of Dreams, appears in *The Pilgrims on the Rhine.* The narrator is a German student and the story is a fiction he has written as part of his study on the history of religion. Before beginning his tale the German notes: 'by a constant reference to the early records of human learning, I have studied to weave it up from truths.' He goes on to recite the story as it is here.

161

1   Bulwer makes a rather blunt note in his text here: The *critic will perceive that this sketch of the beast. Whose race has perished, is mainly cast to designate the remote period of the world in which the tale is told.*

2   **giants in that day:** Bulwer, always a thorough researcher in his work, here alludes to the Celtic legend that Britain was originally inhabited by a race of giants. Arthur and his men are sometimes described as being much larger than modern men and Geoffrey of Monmouth in his *History of the kings of Britain* claims that the last giant Gogmagog, was defeated by Corineus, a Trojan settler in Britain.

THE LIFE OF DREAMS

This story, along with The Fallen Star, is taken from the novel, *The Pilgrims of the Rhine.* It is narrated by Trevelyan, the chief male character in the book, after he and his ailing lover Gertrude and her father Vane have left Niederlahstein on their trip up the river. The conversation among them turns to dreams and Trevelyan notes that he:

"once fell in with a singular enthusiast who had taught himself what he described as 'A System of Dreaming'. When he first spoke to me upon it I asked him to explain what he meant which he did somewhat in the following words." The tale is then retold as it appears here.

1   **Falernian:** a famous wine of Falernus in Italy, frequently eulogised by Horace in his *Odes*.

gryphon and the gnome: The gryphon or griffin is remembered in myth as a fabulous creature with a lion's body, huge wings and an eagle's head. The Greeks regarded them as sacred to the god Apollo, whose treasure they guarded. Gnomes were originally dwarfish spirits of a subterranean race who also guarded treasure, usually buried in the depths of the earth.

sounded the horn at enchanted portals: In Celtic tradition a horn is often sounded at a sacred spot after a hero has